Alaska Assassins

An Olive Reader Mystery

by

L. V. Nield

Copyright © 2019 by L. V. Nield

For information, email Cozy Cat Press, cozycatpress@aol.com or visit our website at: www.cozycatpress.com

COZY CAT
PRESS

ISBN: 978-1-946063-84-7
Printed in the United States of America

10 9 8 7 6 5 4 3 2 1

ACKNOWLEDGMENTS

As Always, my deepest thanks to my husband, Dave Somerfield, for his early reading and constant encouragement of my efforts. Friends' advice in making plot changes was so helpful. Thanks to Debbie Goodridge here at home, and Sue and Chris Aronson and Kay Kos, who all bounced around ideas with me while sitting on the beach in Thailand.

To Patricia Rockwell of Cozy Cat Press, whose timely comments, faith in the story and decision to publish it, I offer my sincere gratitude. Thanks also to Blair Beeston for her help in inputting and formatting the manuscript.

In 2015 my husband and I took a seven day cruise to Alaska on the Holland America Line from Vancouver, Canada. My journal entries and photos from the trip provided great memories of Holland America's impeccable hospitality and the beauty of Alaska. Any errors included in this novel are mine alone. Finally, my thanks to Bonnie Johnston, a travel agent extraordinaire with Marlin Travel of Nanaimo, for her work in setting up our cruise, and her timely reminders in recreating the cruise for this novel.

IN MEMORY OF

My mother, Mae Currie Nield
(1927 – 1983)

AND

My mother-in-law, Beatrice Hinze Somerfield
(1922 – 1987)

These great women would have loved an exciting cruise
to Alaska.

Chapter 1

Olive and her husband, Howard, were taking a quiet stroll along Willow Street in Wantagh, Long Island, enjoying the late June sunshine and each other. Even though Long Island itself was heavily populated, this little street was like many in the residential part of Wantagh; the homes here were often identical, built post-war for returning veterans. This was where Howard and his first wife, Winnie, long deceased, had lived all through their marriage.

When Olive first moved into their home, she'd had to deal with the guilt that she could not help but feel, knowing that she would be taking the place of Howard's first love. But then Howard had reminded her that he knew that Bill had been Olive's own first love. They should both think of their marriage as an adventure, he said—this was a new chapter in their lives.

"I can't believe it will be our first anniversary in August!" Olive exclaimed softly, and Howard bent down to give her a peck on the cheek. Their wedding last year had been a quiet affair, the August day not too humid, with her twin sister Jean, and Jean's sister-in-law, Maggie, as their witnesses in the chapel at the New York retirement home, Flushing Meadows, where they had all three lived at the time. Olive had moved to the home in Queens to be with Jean only a year prior, after puttering around on the old farm for a year without Bill, her late husband.

Olive's son Jon and his wife, Karen, had come from North Dakota to New York in July, after the wheat had been planted on the farm, which Jon had taken over. Olive knew that her son was happy about her upcoming union with Howard. When they all recounted their misadventures with the lawyer, Barnes, Jon had told Howard, "You are one brave dude!" As Howard had done in telling Olive about his war service, he had also downplayed his part in "that Kinfolk thing," as he called it, which only made Jon admire him all the more.

The Barnes business had begun a year ago, when Olive started volunteering at the nursing home next to Flushing Meadows, where she'd met Howard—and also unfortunately, a lawyer intent on scamming older folks without any next of kin into leaving him all their money before ending their lives. With Jean and Maggie at her side, Olive had taken down Barnes to protect Howard from the lawyer's dastardly plans; although the affair almost cost them their lives, Olive and Howard developed an unbreakable bond.

On hearing this, Jon was initially very concerned about Olive's shenanigans in the Big Apple, but after seeing Howard's devotion and fierce protectiveness of his fiancée, he decided his mother was in good hands. Because of the upcoming harvest, Jon and Karen couldn't come back for the wedding, but instead sent a heartfelt card and a gift certificate for a high-end Manhattan hotel, which Olive and Howard decided to use for their honeymoon. The co-conspirators Jean and Maggie had added tickets to a Broadway matinee, so it was just perfect.

Shortly after Howard's proposal, Olive and Howard had moved into his old home in Wantagh. While she would miss the perks of living at Flushing Meadows—meals prepared and served in the dining room, the volunteer work at the nursing home, frequent outings with Jean and Maggie—Olive loved waking up with a contented sense of well-being, looking across the bed at Howard's still-sleeping frame. And she still got together with Maggie and Jean pretty frequently, although as of late they'd been seeing a little less of each other.

"You're thinking about Maggie and Jean, aren't you?" Howard said.

Startled, Olive looked up into Howard's kind eyes. "How could you tell?" she asked, somewhat flustered.

"You get a little wrinkle between your eyes whenever you miss them," he chuckled. "As it happens, I checked the Yankees' schedule, and it looks like Thursday is a travel day. That would be a good time to invite Maggie and Jean for dinner and an overnight stay without sacrificing time with their beloved Bronx Bombers."

Olive smiled. "That is so thoughtful! We can put something on the grill," she said, beginning to get excited. "It will all be a nice change from the Flushing Meadows menu." For Olive, the novelty of having dinner prepared for her had worn off quickly, especially since the menu tended to repeat itself month after month.

"We'll pick them up at the train station, like usual?" Howard asked. While Howard and Olive typically used public transit when going into Manhattan, they enjoyed having Howard's car for local errands. Howard had insisted that Olive get comfortable with driving in Wantagh; even though traffic there was certainly more intimidating than Grafton, North Dakota, it really helped for appointments with the doctor or the physiotherapist, as Olive could just let Howard off at the door. He was still slowly recovering from the stroke that had originally put him in the nursing home next to Flushing Meadows.

"Sounds like a plan!" Olive responded.

"Great. I'll give Jean a call when we get back to the house," Howard promised. "In the meantime, let's just enjoy our walk."

Olive heartily agreed and pressed closer to Howard as they wandered down the sidewalk. A lot had happened in the past three years, but with Howard by her side, she felt invincible.

Chapter 2

As always, Jean and Maggie provided endless entertainment for Howard. He chuckled to himself as he observed them gesturing animatedly on the patio. They'd eagerly accepted the invitation for dinner and an overnight on Thursday.

Talking over one another, loud and boisterous, Jean and Maggie were more like twin sisters than Olive and Jean, Howard thought. Both Maggie and Jean used hair dye liberally and obviously, while Olive, like Howard's late wife Winnie, sported a natural gray-going-on white coif, which was beautiful, framing her soft skin and keeping with her quiet, wry manner.

Standing next to the grill, Jean was talking excitedly about the season the Yankees were having, "playing like they meant it" this year. Howard enjoyed the excitement of baseball in person, but not so much on television—although he was known to rail at the television when cheering for his Rangers during hockey season. Olive had come to enjoy those games as well, more out of sentimentality than interest in hockey, remembering Howard teaching her the finer points of hockey when he was a patient in the nursing home. She did see what he meant about live baseball, though, and this year they had actually taken in two Yankees' games and one Mets' game live.

Howard bought rib eye steaks for the occasion, and Olive baked some potatoes, complementing them with fresh peas and salad, all from her garden. She was enjoying cooking again, having gotten out of the habit because of the preselected menu at Flushing Meadows. She did, however, acknowledge that the occasion warranted the purchase of a cheesecake from the local bakery, and Maggie had brought a bottle of cabernet to pair with the steak.

Howard was nursing his scotch while the women all sipped beer, and Jean was looking in rapt attention at the steaks sizzling on the grill. "So, are you two planning a getaway for your first anniversary?" she asked, eyes still on the steaks.

Olive just shrugged. "We haven't really talked about it. It seems like this whole year has been a getaway for me, with Howard getting healthier every week and us enjoying our yard and garden."

"Speak for yourself, young lady!" Howard exclaimed. "Actually, I'm glad we're getting together with these two fine women, as I have indeed been planning a getaway. And I will now tell you about it."

In response to the puzzled looks from the women, Howard reached back and produced three pamphlets from the table near the door. He handed them out, and the women stared at each other and the pamphlets in amazement.

"An Alaskan cruise!" Jean blurted out. "Olive, you lucky soul!"

"Oh, Howard. That's a long flight to the West Coast." Olive gestured anxiously. "Maybe we should wait until next year?"

"Who said I was going?" Howard grinned. "I already talked to the travel agent and I can get the three of you on a mid-August cruise. It will be seven days from Vancouver on the Inside Passage along the coast to the south of Alaska, with lots to do on board, and some great land excursions, too. And I won't be talked out of it. I already put down a deposit, so there you have it.

And it's my treat, airfare and all. I can't tell you the fun I've had planning this."

The women just stood and stared at Howard.

He shook his head slowly and took a sip of his scotch. "I can't believe I've been able to render Jean and Maggie speechless," he chuckled.

Rousing themselves, the women all began talking at once: "But you'll be alone while we're off traveling!" "Don't you want to take the trip, too?" "How will you manage?" "It's all so expensive!"

Howard just raised his hand to stop the chatter. "The steaks are done, so let's go inside," he announced. "We'll talk more about the itinerary over cheesecake, but I don't want to hear another word about whether or not you're going! Olive gave me the greatest gift a man can hope for when she agreed to be my wife. Winnie and I traveled all over during our younger years, but Olive never had the chance. She and I'll take the next one together, but for now, it will be a great experience for all of you to share. So there. Let's eat!"

Chapter 3

Sitting in a row of seats on the flight to Vancouver, the three women looked at each other, still a little incredulous.

The weeks leading up to the flight had been a whirlwind. The women had all applied for and received passports. "You *are* going through another country, you know," Howard had said in response to their protests. "And who knows, if Olive likes this cruise, we may decide to cruise to Cuba, if that whole situation ever gets sorted out."

The meeting with the travel agent, Bonnie, had been a blast. Since she had taken the same Alaskan cruise a couple of years earlier, Bonnie was a great source of information about the routines aboard ship and the choice of shore excursions offered in each port of call. She told them that the weather in August could be changeable along the coast, and suggested packing layers of clothing to suit both muggy, warm days and cooler, rainy evenings. Jean, Maggie, and Olive had enthusiastically agreed to try the helicopter ride to the large glacier outside of Juneau, which was their first port of call. The excursions all cost extra and Maggie and Jean had insisted on paying for them, but Howard wouldn't hear of it; he had told Bonnie beforehand that the cost was between her and him. Of course, because he didn't bother with computers, he hadn't realized that Maggie and Jean could see on the Holland America cruise website what a tremendous gift he was giving them.

Bonnie asked the women if they had any evening wear, and in response to their blank stares, she'd advised that they each buy a simple floor-length skirt and a couple of blouses, as the dining room had a dress code, and a stricter one on gala nights. None of the women had dressed up like that in years, so an afternoon spent shopping was just part of the anticipation. Howard had grinned when Olive came home with her purchases, eager to show them off to him.

Jean now looked out the window of the plane and then over at Olive. "I can't believe we've never flown together before," she said. "Let me know when we fly over North Dakota, will you?"

"Very funny." Olive grimaced and gave Jean a well-deserved pinch. "I get tired of all those kinds of comments on the news, as though the world begins and ends in New York!"

Maggie decided to intervene. "Well, for our purposes, the world this week begins and ends in Vancouver, believe it or not, with a big chunk of fun in Alaska in between."

From the moment the women got off the plane, they were impressed with Vancouver. "Watching the Winter Olympic Games last year, the city looked like some kind of paradise, but this is . . . wow!" Jean blurted out as they walked by the Native sculptures on their way to the baggage area. "Even the Customs people were nice!" Maggie answered.

While Maggie and Olive waited by the baggage carousel, Jean used the courtesy phone to call for the shuttle to the hotel. Emerging into the sunshine with their bags, they were soon on their way from the airport, giggling like schoolgirls at the passing scenery.

The driver must have noticed, because he called out, "First time in Vancouver?" from the front seat.

Arriving at the Pan Pacific Hotel around one o'clock, they were stunned by the beauty of the hotel itself and, of course, its surroundings. The roof was adorned with huge sails, making it look like a ship, and there were cruise ships actually docked right beside it in the harbor. Howard had booked them a room for that night and the next to allow the women enough time for sight seeing and to acclimate to the three-hour time difference.

Their plan now was to freshen up and then venture out along the harbor walkway as far as the area known as Gastown. Maggie and Jean had surfed the net a lot in the past couple of weeks to search for interesting things to see along the trip. The next day, they planned to take a trolley tour around the city. Additionally, the hotel lobby had a whole display of attractions and a walking map.

When they opened the door to their room, however, they let out a collective gasp.

"Does your husband have a money tree somewhere on Long Island?" Maggie shouted, while Jean gave Olive a bear hug.

"When we get back I'm going to give that guy a big kiss on the lips!" Jean exclaimed.

"Well, he is a very good kisser!" Olive giggled, blushing a little.

The suite had floor-to-ceiling windows with a view of the harbor on one side and a view of the shore on the other.

Maggie opened up the map and pointed out the window. "That's the Lion's Gate Bridge to the northwest, and that's North Vancouver across the water."

"Come on, let's go!" Jean, always restless, wanted to see the sights. They followed her to the elevator and out the door, enjoying the blue of the water against the bright, sunny sky.

Gastown did not disappoint. There were art galleries and shops, a steam-powered clock, and a statue of "Gassy Jack." They spent almost an hour going through a huge store that sold Native crafts and clothing.

"We have to shop here after the cruise so I can buy Howard a Cowichan wool sweater," Olive said. "It's so soft, and apparently it's good in rainy weather." She showed Jean one of the knitted outdoor sweaters created by Native women on Vancouver Island, which was just fifty miles or so across the Georgia Strait.

As they walked around Gastown, they looked out over the waterfront, seeing some vestiges of the port it must have been, almost now completely supplanted by tourist attractions, office buildings, restaurants, and a small ferry terminal for the passenger ferry to the North Shore. They looked east and saw what appeared to be a less touristy area—kind of seedy, really—and then back toward the water adjacent to it, with its railway tracks and more industrial setting. *Probably not on the tourist brochures,* Olive thought.

By four o'clock, all the air travel and walking had left them ready for a shower, a cold beverage in the bar, and some dinner on the outdoor terrace of the hotel.

Chapter 4

"Christ on a bicycle, what a set-up!" Jean exclaimed as the women walked into hotel bar. Refreshed by their short rest in the hotel room after their showers, Maggie had led them in search of what she termed "an adult beverage," and Jean and Olive weren't about to argue. With soft music playing in the background and a few patrons murmuring at tables looking out on the harbor, Olive ventured that the bar would be the perfect place to talk over their plans for the following day.

Hearing some loud voices, the ladies turned to see two couples make their way over to the area where they had intended to sit. Both men were wearing ball hats with the New York Yankees logo on them, and their wives were resplendent in bright summer dresses.

After they sat down, Jean walked over to the table next to theirs and greeted them: "Ah, fellow Yankee fans! Maggie and I are blown away with the kind of season they're having."

"Same with us! To bounce back after last season is just great," said the taller of the two men.

As Olive and Maggie joined Jean at the adjacent table, Maggie piped up, "Oh to be Mets fans these days! They've got nothing to cheer for."

The other man chortled and signaled to the server. The wives just looked on, nodding, but saying nothing. They probably weren't very interested in sports.

"We didn't think we'd see any Yankee fans this far west in Canada, but maybe people out here don't like Toronto any more than folks in the Midwest aren't thrilled with New Yorkers," Maggie continued. "Am I right, Olive?" Olive was startled to hear Maggie call her name, but just smiled in response. She wasn't very interested in sports, either.

"So you ladies are American, too?" the bigger man asked. He gestured to his own group. "We're from Westchester County, just outside of Manhattan."

"My sister, Olive, just moved to Queens from North Dakota a couple of years ago and now lives on Long Island, while Maggie and I have lived in Queens for many years," Jean responded. "I'm Jean, by the way."

"My name is Jack Leonard and this is my wife, Karen," the bigger man countered, pointing to the woman on his right. Then, touching the shoulder of the woman on his left, he added, "And this is Bev Harrington and her husband, Art. They live in the same neighborhood as us and belong to the same country club."

Bev then spoke up. "So what brings all of you to Vancouver?" Her voice had a smoker's gravelly huskiness to it, and she spoke somewhat louder than needed, given the proximity of the tables. "This trip was Karen's bright idea, and my husband here thought it would be good to come along. I'm not so sure, but here we are . . ." Her voice trailed off as she gave a sour look at Jack's wife.

"Come on, Bev, the cruise should be wonderful!" Art piped up.

"Yeah, and Jack and I are both missing prime golf weather back home!" Bev shot back.

Olive sat forward, somewhat stunned by Bev's negative attitude. "We're going on the cruise too, and it should be a real adventure," she said. "It's a first anniversary gift from my husband, so we plan to make the most of it and report back to him."

"Well, I never!" Bev sneered. "Your husband buys you all a trip and then doesn't come along? I should have bought the trip for Art. It would have worked out better."

Olive felt the color rise up her neck. "I wanted him to come, but he's still recovering from a stroke and didn't want to risk it. It was a wonderful gesture to pay for a trip for all of us to enjoy."

An awkward silence fell over the group until Karen interjected, "I've always wanted to go to Alaska and everyone who's been on the cruise spoke so highly of it."

Art nodded. "I can't wait to do some hiking in some real wilderness, not the small parks that pass for nature in Westchester."

Jack reached over to slap Art on the knee. "I've told you that if you just took up golf with your good wife and me, you'd get all the nature you'll ever need. I just agreed to go along on this thing to get Karen off my back," he said, rolling his eyes. "And anyhow, dinner and a show should be all a woman needs to celebrate an anniversary!"

Again, an awkward silence.

Karen looked at Olive. "So, what are your plans for tomorrow?" she asked kindly.

Olive gazed outside the window and told Karen about their plans for the trolley excursion around the city, still stung by Jack and Bev's comments.

Jack snorted. "This looks like one backwater town to me. I watched some of the Winter Olympics last year, and all they could do was gush about the water and the mountains. Bo-ring! And these Canadians! All they know is hockey and curling. Curling, for heaven's sake! Sliding down the ice with a broom in your hand? I'll take a day on the golf course any time."

Karen looked over at her husband. "I actually want to go on that trolley ride to get to know Vancouver better," she said. "I read the brochure for it in the lobby and it looks fascinating."

Jack snorted a second time. "Oh, for heaven's sake, we'll see enough 'fascinating' things on the cruise. Count me out!"

Bev joined in. "That's not for me, either. I don't mind seeing stuff in Alaska, but I could care less about Vancouver."

Art sat in silence for a moment before he looked over at Olive and asked, "I'd like to go on the trolley, too, so if you don't mind, Karen and I could join you ladies to see the sights?"

Olive nodded and Jean added, "Sure, we can get to know each other before we set sail!"

Chapter 5

"Oh, that trolley is so cute—just like the ones they show in movies about San Francisco!" Olive and Jean exclaimed in unison, and then laughed as Maggie rolled her eyes.

Other visitors to Vancouver had already boarded the trolley for the tour. They nodded to an Asian man sitting alone with a camera, who merely responded with a neutral expression, so they turned to a young couple who greeted them with big smiles and "G'day ladies." *Obviously from Australia,* Olive thought as the women waited to board themselves.

A nice-looking young fellow had alighted from the vehicle, taking their tickets. "I was told there would be four people getting on at this stop?" The young man looked around as he directed the women onto the trolley. "We've got time, so I'll wait a couple of minutes."

At that moment, Olive heard the sound of Jack Leonard's voice, as strident as it had been the day before. Looking through the windows of the trolley, she saw both couples, rather than just Karen Leonard and Art Herrington. Secretly hoping that Jack had not had a change of heart—he would really fill up the trolley in a hurry—she sighed. But all became clear when the tour guide asked how many were in their party.

"Naw," Jack shouted back. "I just came this far to smoke my cigar. You can't smoke anywhere around here. I heard Canadians were big on rules, but come on!"

Olive could see Karen gritting her teeth as she boarded the trolley, with Art following behind. They sat down near the three ladies. As Jack and Bev walked away, Karen let out a long-held breath while Art just sat back and closed his eyes.

Opening them again, he nodded to the women. "Did any of you ever smoke?" he asked. Seeing them shake their heads, he muttered, "I keep trying to get Bev to give up cigarettes—and, Karen, I don't understand how you can put up with those cigars of Jack's. They look like dirigibles and smell like bonfires."

Karen nodded in agreement. "I've tried to get him to stop smoking in the house, but 'a man's home is his castle' and all that. Luckily, Jack Jr. hasn't taken up the habit. When Jack comes home from golf, it just wafts in the front door with him."

Olive, Jean, and Maggie all exchanged glances, wordlessly agreeing that the cruise was probably the last thing these two couples should have undertaken. Following their drink in the bar yesterday, Jack had announced that he was ready for a steak and the couples had walked out, apparently to an expensive local steakhouse. The women had decided to sit and enjoy a second cocktail before adjourning to a quiet dinner on the terrace at the hotel.

The trolley tour was everything Olive had hoped it would be. When she telephoned Howard from the airport the previous day, she'd promised to call him this afternoon to report, bearing in mind the three-hour time difference. She knew she would have a hard time describing all of the sights, so she planned to take a lot of photos.

The trolley wound its way through Stanley Park in the west end of the city, stopping along the way. They could get off at any stop and then jump back on when the next trolley came by. The women had already looked at the brochure and, realizing that it had 20 stops, knew they couldn't "jump off" at every one.

Seeing the aquarium, Olive sighed. Oh, to have more time! The young trolley guide told them that the aquarium had thirty exhibits, including dolphin shows, sharks in underwater tanks, and seals and otters.

The next stop was equally tempting, as it featured nine huge totem poles, carved by artisans around British Columbia. The poles featured human and animal forms piled one on top of the other, all quite imposing and painted in different hues. From the trolley, Olive could also see large sculptures; the guide described one in particular, a raven carved into a huge Douglas fir stump. Maggie reminded them that at a stop on the cruise they would see a similar exhibit, so they stayed on the trolley, while the Australian couple jumped off with a quick wave and a "nice to meet ya."

Both Prospect Point and Ferguson Point afforded them breathtaking views—the first one of the inlet and the second of the ocean.

The seawall was another point of interest, running parallel to the beach and obviously a favorite path of cyclists and joggers. "Imagine living here!" Olive exclaimed. "A warm climate and parks like this! I thought Central Park in Manhattan was special, but this is really something. No wonder so many people around here look so healthy and fit."

The women had discussed the next two stops, the Museum of Vancouver and the Maritime Museum of British Columbia. They knew that, given their time constraints, they would have to choose between the two museums. The guide told them that the Museum of Vancouver had opened in 1894 with some collectibles from around the world which the founders thought the locals should see. Over time the concept had changed, so that now it was a celebration of the culture in

Vancouver through history. While that sounded really interesting, Maggie was curious about the Maritime Museum—"sounds like something practical, not too artsy"—so the whole group decided to jump off there.

Just as they began to walk to the building, Olive noticed that the man with the camera also quickly departed the trolley and walked a short distance behind Karen and Art, while studiously looking elsewhere. She thought of asking him to join the group, but figured he probably didn't need their company to enjoy himself.

The museum turned out to be fascinating. The St. Roche, a boat used in the Arctic from 1928 to 1954, was amazing. Karen blurted out, "If Jack had come along he would have really liked this!" The St. Roche's voyages were long and difficult, and in very cramped quarters, but they'd helped confirm Canadian sovereignty in the area. Their museum tour also included information about the ill-fated Franklin expedition, in which all hands had died trying to find the Northwest Passage in the 1700s. Olive shuddered to think of the hardship of winter in the Arctic, and the long, slow death surely experienced by the crew.

They wandered out of the building, and, spotting a trolley coming down the street, walked quickly toward the stop. As it pulled away, the man with the camera jumped on it and again took a seat away from the other riders. Olive wondered wryly whether he would jump on and off with them for the balance of the tour, and, sure enough, he disembarked at Granville Island with them, too, only to melt into the crowd.

Jean had already "penciled in" the next stop at Granville Island so they could visit the brewpub there. She got no argument from either Olive or Maggie, and Karen and Art were happy to tag along. The Island housed more than the brewpub; while it had started out years ago as an industrial site, it had been transformed into a wonderful destination for tourists and locals alike. The women wandered through the Granville Island Market, and were astounded by the array of fresh fruits and vegetables, as well as the many wonderful handmade items for sale. Leaving the covered portion, they ventured through the walking area, past jugglers and other street entertainers, taking note of the signs for live theatre.

"Christ on a bicycle!" Jean almost shouted, "They even have a university here!" She gestured toward the sign for the Emily Carr School of Fine Art.

The five of them looked ahead and saw a welcome sight: The Granville Island Brewing Company.

Art let out a laugh. "The first round is on me!"

The women found themselves enjoying Karen and Art's company. Once their respective spouses had walked off at the beginning of the tour, both seemed to relax and take in the sights.

"You seem very fit. Do you work out a lot?" Maggie asked Art.

He thanked her for the compliment. "I love hiking, and did a lot of it with my son when he was younger," he explained. "We always tried to interest Bev, but she went a few times and made it clear that any time spared for that meant less time for golf lessons and playing. Neither my son nor I were ever very interested in golf. He lives in Boston now, but if he comes home for the holidays, we try to get out for an afternoon. I do weights at home and have a treadmill to strengthen my body for the hike—some of the trails are pretty daunting. I'm planning to get outdoors at Skagway. Apparently, Bev and Jack have already booked a golf game there."

Jean looked at Karen. "You are so petite—especially next to Jack, who's such a big guy!" she said, with all of her usual tact. "How did you meet, if you don't mind me asking?"

Karen's look was almost rueful. "I was a freshman at Hofstra and Jack was a sophomore, playing tight end for the football team," she said. "One evening, at a function, he came over and introduced himself. I was quite flattered, as I knew his name and that he had a chance to go pro. He was handsome and affable, and appeared to be popular, so it was surprising that he'd even look at me."

"I've known him ever since Jack and Karen moved into our neighborhood, so I'll warn you in advance," Art interjected. "He will give any new person he meets the whole chapter and verse about his knee injury and how he could have been an All-Pro tight end. And how the injury kept him out of Vietnam, too, which is a little contradictory, but Jack is a man of contradictions, for sure. Bev and I are a few years younger than Jack, so Vietnam wasn't an issue for me." He paused and gave Karen a sheepish look. "Sorry, Karen—I shouldn't tell tales on your husband, but he's been acting like a jerk lately."

"Well, hopefully he'll get over it," Karen sighed. "Jack Jr. has even noticed it, as though his father thinks he's missed out on something."

Refreshed by the cold beer, the five of them caught the trolley, again joined by the Camera Man, as Olive now secretly referred to him, and passed through the "sports district,' which housed BC Place, a huge stadium used for both football and soccer, and Rogers Arena, used by the Vancouver Canucks hockey team in the winter months. The trolley guide also pointed out the Queen Elizabeth Theatre, which hosted many touring Broadway shows and mainstream concerts.

"So much for 'backwater,' Jack," Art muttered.

The next trolley stop, Chinatown, looked interesting, especially the Sun Yat Sen Garden, but Karen and Art wanted to jump off at Gastown instead. As the women had already been to Gastown, they decided to leave Art and Karen at the stop and continue back to the hotel. Olive noticed that the Camera Man waited until the couple had left the trolley before jumping off himself and walking a distance behind them.

When Jean and Maggie remembered on the walk back that the Yankees were playing a game against the Toronto Blue Jays that night—meaning that it would be broadcast at four o'clock in Vancouver—they were ecstatic. They didn't want to hurt Olive's feelings, especially since Howard had been nice enough to pay for the whole trip, so they told her they'd be fine watching the later innings after dining out somewhere.

Olive surprised them. "I don't care if we eat out, as we'll have lots of food on the cruise, and I don't mind watching the game with you," she said. "If I get tired, I can always put in my earphones and read something. I saw some food trucks near Canada Place, and there's a liquor store nearby, so why don't we just buy some beer and eat take-out in our room?"

"You are such a doll!" Jean and Maggie squealed in unison, and nearly crushed Olive in their bear hug.

Chapter 6

"Today's the day!" Jean grinned as she looked out the window onto the Holland American cruise ship that had pulled up into the slip beside the hotel. "That puppy is huge!"

Maggie yawned while brewing a cup of coffee. "I actually read about the ship in the brochure from the travel agent," she said. "It's just the right size and holds about fourteen-hundred passengers—not like those humongous ones that carry about four thousand people around the Caribbean. There will be some kids on board, but we shouldn't be overrun by them, and apparently they have special play areas for them, too."

Olive giggled. "Let's get Howard on the phone and we'll all say goodbye together," she suggested. "We probably won't be able to call him until we get back, although maybe when we're in port we can. But I don't want him to expect to hear from me during the cruise itself!"

Since they couldn't board until after noon, they decided to take a walk outside to see the ship from a different angle, and then grab a bagel or muffin at a coffee house they had seen on their walk the previous day.

Getting off the elevator, they spied Jack shaking his finger at Karen, telling her in an irritated voice, "Look, I've already told you. I'm not going on the stupid train trip out of Skagway. Bev and I plan to golf, so you can just invite yourself along with those other old broads from New York."

Olive motioned for Jean and Maggie to stop for a moment, hoping that Karen wouldn't see them. She could feel Karen's embarrassment and frustration from all the way across the lobby. Luckily, Jack moved on ahead toward the check-out so the women could slip outside unnoticed.

"Let's make sure we invite her along on the train," Jean muttered. "This cruise was going to be more about us, but if Karen's been looking forward to this time with her husband, it looks like she can forget it. And you'd think Bev would be a little empathetic with Karen, but then again, she doesn't seem to want to do much with Art, either."

Maggie added, "I ran into Art after he and Karen finished the trolley tour, and he specifically asked if we could join their group for dinner a couple of times. He said that both he and Karen had enjoyed our company on the trolley, and since Bev and Karen had little in common, it would be a nice break for her to converse with all of us. He said he'd 'run interference' with Jack so that Karen could get a word in edgewise."

Olive looked off into the distance. "I wonder if Jack and Bev don't have something going on," she murmured.

Maggie and Jean just gaped at her.

"Little sister, I can't imagine you coming out with something like that!" Jean accused.

Olive just grinned. "I didn't fall off the turnip truck, you know. I'll keep an eye out."

Maggie took Olive by the shoulders. "Remember the last thing that Howard said before he put us in the taxi to the airport? Remember, dear girl? He said, and repeat after me: 'Olive, you will not do any sleuthing during the trip!' He also reminded you that we were *all* in harm's way during the Kinfolk thing, so you are to *mind your own business*. And you will, isn't that right?"

"Yes, of course." Olive mollified both Jean and Maggie by crossing her heart.

Noon found the women standing in a line with many others, handing off their luggage to be taken to their suite. Olive began looking around, commenting to Jean that the travelers around them were of varying ages; just ahead of them stood a much older woman and a younger Asian woman holding their passports and tickets. The older woman identified herself to the cruise representative as Countess Von Holbein, and then motioned to the younger woman to hand over the documents. Once that was completed, she curtly barked to her companion, "Come, don't dawdle," in a heavy Russian accent, to which her companion mutely nodded. She trailed quickly after "the Countess," who by that time had strode ahead.

Maggie and Jean had also witnessed the exchange, and looked at Olive with raised eyebrows. Royalty, indeed!

Realizing that the cruise representative was beckoning them to step forward, the women immediately complied, bringing their passports and tickets out of their purses. After showing their identification, they obtained cards to their suite and listened to the cruise employee's admonishment to *not in any circumstance* lose track of the cards. They were required not only in order to get off, but, more importantly, to get back on board the ship after an excursion. They all nodded solemnly before almost skipping through the passageway onto the lower deck. The ship was scheduled to set sail at four, so they had ample time to explore and look out at the shoreline.

Letting themselves into the suite, they gasped at its splendor. Jean couldn't help herself: "My new brother-in-law now will receive *two* kisses right on the lips when we get home! Now, let's take some photos while the place still looks this neat."

As with the room at the Pan Pacific, the suite, called "The Neptune," had two beds and a pull-out sofa bed in the sitting area. There was a whirlpool tub in the bathroom, and the veranda noticeably extended the size of the room. Howard had also thoughtfully pre-ordered some wine and scotch for their suite so that they could enjoy a glass while savoring the view, and at much less cost than room service.

"Since our luggage hasn't been delivered yet, there's no need to stick around and unpack, so let's look around," Jean ventured, still gazing out the veranda. "When the ship leaves we should probably be out on the top deck anyway, so we can get a 360-degree view of everything."

Maggie and Olive nodded in agreement, and the trio shortly left the room for the elevator.

They started by going to the very top deck and working their way down. The ship seemed to have everything, including a nightclub. Another floor with a retractable roof housed a large pool and two hot tubs, and along the perimeter there were plenty of reclining deck chairs, with fast food and beverages on offer already. Walking away from that area, they spied a huge buffet, with tables along the windows, where they would be able to order breakfast, lunch, and even dinner if they didn't want to use the more formal dining room.

"I bet this place is busy in the mornings," Maggie observed. "I also bet a lot of parents bring their kids here for dinner, too."

"I sure hope so!" Olive exclaimed, knowing they were going to eat in the dining room. "I'll feel blessed if Jon and Karen give me a grandchild, but right now

I'd prefer a quiet dinner without the noise of restless children."

"Speaking of," Jean guffawed, "look who's coming!"

Sure enough, just as the women turned, in strolled Jack Leonard, waving his hands and shouting something at Art.

Karen waved to the women, so they walked toward the other party. "We've just been on another floor where they've got the dining room; we couldn't see in because it doesn't open till later, but I bet it's beautiful," Karen said excitedly. "Then there's a lounge for jazz and dancing, and right beside it, a kind of pub where they have early evening quizzes and a performance by a guitarist every night—at least according to the sign. They even have a small casino, although that doesn't really interest me."

"Speak for yourself, Karen!" Jack brayed over her. "I gave up quizzes when I finished school. I'm going to check out the casino when it opens tonight, so I plan to go for the early sitting at dinner. I assume they know how to cook steak, although the workers all look like they come from Asia or some other place."

Jack appeared to have the unerring ability to cause uncomfortable silences, which he obliviously filled by continuing his blather. Luckily, Art interjected, "I'm not much on gambling, but going for an earlier dinner and trying the quiz sounds like a great evening. Would you ladies like to join us for dinner, say, at six o'clock? The ship will have left the harbor, and we'd be more likely to get a window seat, I hope."

Caught off-guard, the women hesitated, but, not wanting to embarrass Art, Olive spoke up, saying that would be fine. "We'll just meet you at the entrance," she said.

They left the two couples and continued their tour of the ship. They soon came upon the pub that Karen had spoken about, and Jean plopped herself down in a chair and called to the bartender, "Is it too early for a beverage?"

Over a glass of beer, each of the women shook their heads, marveling at how obtuse Jack could be. "Let's just give dinner a try tonight, and if he's still a jerk, we can get our own table tomorrow," Olive said ruefully.

As they were finishing their beer, they spotted a young couple walking toward their table. "Why, it's the Australians from the trolley tour!" Jean waved to them to say hello.

The couple waved back and approached the women's table. "We didn't realize you all would also be on the cruise!" the young man exclaimed.

"Is this your first cruise? It's a new experience for us," Jean said. "I'm Jean and this is my sister, Olive, and my sister-in-law, Maggie."

The young woman responded, "My name is Alice and this is my husband, Arnie. We're just waiting for our luggage, so we thought we'd explore the ship a little. That beer looks like a great idea. We Aussies love our beer!"

Arnie chuckled. "My bride speaks the truth for sure, although we're both feeling a little under the weather. We're meeting up with some of my old college chums, so I hope this bug or jet lag or whatever it is doesn't last too long."

"So you've flown all the way from Australia to take this cruise?" Jean asked. "It seems like a long way for a college reunion, although that's kind of a cool idea all the same."

Alice grinned. "Actually, Arnie's mates came to Canada earlier and have been to the Rockies and some other places in North America," she explained. "We just flew in from Africa a couple of days ago so we could explore Vancouver before boarding today."

"Africa!" Olive gasped. "From the heat of that continent to wearing heavy sweaters in Alaska—you two are adventurers! What took you there?"

"I'm a nurse, and Arnie and I both worked in a village in Gabon," Alice replied. "Arnie's part of an NGO trying to bring wells to remote areas, so that people will have clean drinking water. The small clinic in Gabon services a wide area, and we both thought we could do something productive together. But it wears you down, so we're treating ourselves to a much-needed vacation and an adventure in celebrating our first wedding anniversary."

"What you're doing is so admirable," Maggie sighed. "In the States, we hear about young people lacking ambition, which isn't fair at all. You two are a good example of turning caring into sharing."

Arnie laughed. "If you don't mind, I'm going to tell my boss that we should use that slogan in our fundraising!"

Alice and Arnie nodded to each other and stood up. "We're going to try to get a nap before we leave the harbor," Alice said. "Hopefully we can shake this lethargy and get on with the fun!"

Finding their luggage placed in their suite, the women were able to unpack and then go topside to witness the ship's departure from Vancouver. They got into the elevator, which at that point was half-full of passengers, including the Countess and her companion. Both were staring straight ahead, not speaking, although the Countess did respond with a smile when Olive ventured a timid "hello."

Jean murmured to Maggie, "Well, it appears she doesn't bite!"

They all walked out onto the top deck, moving toward the railing for a better view of the shoreline. The Countess again instructed her companion to follow her, causing Olive to quietly remark that the young woman certainly wasn't on this trip for a vacation. She tried to imagine being at someone's beck and call like that, and couldn't fathom it; she would go crazy.

The departure was as glorious as they'd hoped it would be, finding themselves gliding out of the slip, watching Canada Place and the shoreline drift into the distance, and then passing under the Lion's Gate Bridge and into the Georgia Strait. The sea was like glass, and there was no rocking motion at all, nor any worries about motion sickness, so Olive felt like she was standing on her porch. With not a cloud in the sky, the water looked bluer than anything she had ever seen. She took some photos for Howard, but left herself time to just absorb the beauty. Even Maggie and Jean were stunned into silence.

Chapter 7

"Thank goodness the travel agent gave us a heads-up about appropriate attire for the dining room!" Olive exclaimed as she put on her earrings. "I don't mind wearing a long skirt for the gala nights, but I'm glad we can get away with shorter skirts, dresses, or even nice pantsuits on the other evenings."

Jean chimed in, "It was fun to buy the skirts and new blouses, but I still have some nice threads for an evening out, and you know I prefer pantsuits anyway, so this works out great."

"I think we all look presentable, and if we don't, the steward will probably let us know," Maggie added.

The women were on the elevator, not wanting to be late for the six o'clock rendezvous with the two couples. Luckily, they made it to the dining room on time.

Since the couples weren't at the entrance, Olive peered inside, only to spot them at a table near the window, with Karen frantically waving at them. Olive looked at her watch, somewhat piqued that they were, in fact, on time, and that the couples hadn't waited so they could all be seated at the same time. No doubt it had been Jack's decision.

"It appears they're here already," Olive called to Maggie and Jean, who exchanged puzzled looks. Not surprisingly, Jack had given himself and Bev the best seats by the window, across from each other, with Karen seated to his right and Art seated to Bev's left. Fortunately, the windows ran almost floor to ceiling, so that the trio could look past them at the scenery passing by as dusk approached. Jack, it appeared, had already placed his drink order, so the women had to wait for the waiter to return to the table. The travel agent had told them they could order wine by the bottle at the beginning of the cruise, and if it wasn't consumed at the meal, it would be stored for them to enjoy at a later dinner.

"I think I'll splurge and have a martini before dinner," Jean chortled while rubbing her hands together.

Maggie chose a Chivas Regal and Olive said she'd see if the bar had Canadian rye whiskey and ginger ale. Jean looked at Olive and told her that she intended to pay for her own booze during the cruise.

"Too late, I'm afraid." Olive grinned. "The night before we left, Howard told me he had paid extra to make sure we have enough credit with the ship for all the liquor and wine we want—*and* we have to use it up, as it isn't refundable."

Jean gaped at her, sputtering, "Now it's *three* kisses right on the lips!"

The waiter came with drinks for the two couples and took the women's orders. Olive looked around the dining room, noting the quality of the furnishings and efficiency of the personnel. For such a large room and the number of tables, she was surprised that it had a somewhat hushed air. It would have been so romantic—if only Howard had been there!

And then Jack opened his mouth. "So, do you girls get seasick?"

The women shook their heads, although, truth be told, they wouldn't know until they left the shelter of the islands along the Georgia Strait. Bonnie, the travel agent, felt sure that passengers on the Inner Passage cruise had less chance of seasickness because there was little open water.

At that moment, their drinks arrived, and Karen offered up a toast to the trip and to meeting new friends.

"Yeah, yeah," Jack muttered.

He and Bev didn't bother to reach over to their table companions to clink glasses, just raised theirs to each other, exchanging glances.

Then Jack continued to monopolize the conversation. "Well, I don't expect any problems with seasickness. I'm as healthy as a horse!"

The women exchanged their own glances—healthy as a horse's patootie, maybe.

"You see, I was an athlete in my day—a college football recruit, in fact," Jack bragged. "And if I hadn't busted up my knee, I probably would have gone pro!"

Olive watched Karen and Art now look over at her, their silence speaking volumes: *We warned you!*

Art obviously couldn't stand any more, so he asked Jack, "Didn't it keep you out of Vietnam, though?"

Jack almost stood up in rage. "Look, buddy, I was always planning on serving my country!"

Art was now obviously just baiting Jack, and observed aloud that playing pro football wouldn't serve the country.

Jack, infuriated, shot back, "Yeah, well, I'm a damn sight healthier than you are. You have heart problems, Bev tells me, and why you hike like you do is beyond me, as though you're just trying to prove something," he said nastily. "And my wife, what's her problem? Oh, yeah! A nut allergy, for God's sake! Has to carry around one of those pens all the time, and she and I have to spend a bunch of time going through menus and grilling the waiter on what's in this and what's in that. So yeah, I have high cholesterol, but I take medication and life is good. I just get tired of my wife nagging me all the time about exercise and diet, and you acting all superior."

Olive began to wonder if Jack had started drinking his scotch *before* they'd arrived at the dining room, he seemed so loud and belligerent.

Just then the server arrived, so everyone fell silent. Looking over at Art studying his menu, Olive noticed a little smirk. This exchange between the men was not new, obviously, and while Art probably shouldn't have gotten Jack all riled up at the dinner table, she could see why he'd be frustrated listening to Jack alternating between boasts and self-pity.

Looking past Bev, the view from the window was spectacular. Olive nudged Jean, sitting to her right, who whispered to Maggie, seated across from her, "Take a look at that!"

It was growing dark enough that they could see lights starting to twinkle in the various communities along the way. She hadn't realized that Vancouver Island was so huge and that there were smaller islands off *its* coast containing even smaller communities. People must spend most of their time on ferries, she mused, especially if they want to get to the city of Vancouver on the mainland. Intrigued, it occurred to her that, when Howard felt up to travel, wandering around this part of the world would be just the thing to interest him.

Again, Olive was struck by the ambience of the dining room. The flowers, the linens and crystal, the waiters in their spotless, crisp jackets, bending over attentively at each table—Olive had never experienced this! She was happy to enjoy the early sitting, as it left them free for evening activities, but she could see why some couples chose the later sitting, especially if the dinner itself was the focal point of the evening. She nudged Jean again and discreetly pointed toward a table for two, seeing the Countess and her companion being seated, and then watched the pair sit there ignoring each other while perusing their menus.

Then she spotted the Asian man with the camera from the trolley enter the restaurant and sit at a table for two, although he appeared to be alone. He still had his camera strap around his neck! Olive was glad she'd nicknamed him "Camera Man."

Clearly this mode of travel was different from any other she'd experienced. All of these people together, moving toward the same destination. And not a quick air flight, but a leisurely voyage where they might actually speak to one another, although the Countess certainly managed to avoid any intimate conversation with her companion, Olive observed.

Realizing the waiter was next to her elbow, she directed her focus to the menu. All the choices! Determined to try a new food item at every dinner, she ordered "sweetbreads" as an appetizer, a wild mushroom soup to follow, and duck breast as her entrée. She had always liked duck, but sweetbreads, she had no idea.

Art must have picked up on her puzzlement. "They're good, actually. Although, the name doesn't make sense," he explained. "It's actually the thymus gland—not sure if pork or beef—and quick fried."

Bev just looked over at him and sneered. "Well, aren't you the smart one! The only thing good about being a school teacher is a lot of useless information." Her "wit," apparently, was not lost on Jack, who let out a hearty laugh.

Maggie and Jean had already informed Olive that they liked what they liked, so they would probably stick to stuff that they liked. She caught them turning a little green hearing Art's description of sweetbreads, and wasn't surprised to watch them both order the shrimp cocktail, followed by the beef.

Luckily, Jack spent most of the remaining time plowing through his beef so the table was relatively silent for the meal.

The dessert choices were wonderful—cheesecake, torte, or trifle—so the women decided to get one of each and then share before waddling up to their room. They left Jack declaring that he and Bev planned to step out onto the deck to smoke.

Back at the suite, Maggie let out a "Whew! He sure fills a room!"

Jean and Olive nodded as they approached the veranda.

"Let's enjoy the night air ourselves for a few moments and then try the pub to see what the quiz is all about," Olive suggested. "I don't want to miss a thing. And besides, there's music in the pub afterward. I can hold off on listening to the jazz scheduled in the lounge later on until tomorrow evening, as I should get some beauty rest. I'm surprised I'm still a little tired from the time change."

Chapter 8

The Countess glanced around the dining room, ignoring the young Asian woman sitting across the table from her, still wondering if she had done the right thing in bringing her maid with her on this trip. Yes, the girl was helpful at home in Vancouver, kind of all-purpose in her duties, and knowing enough Russian and English to get by, but her presence here soured the Countess' mood.

But the Countess also recognized that she was no longer young—her eighty-five years on this earth attested to that—although she could still walk without assistance and the posture lessons drilled into her by her imperious parents had left her with a straight back.

She had grown up with servants, many from northern China; her parents often "adopted" young Chinese girls, like the young woman sitting across from her now, who had been offered up by families who only wanted sons. Watching her mother instruct the staff, the Countess had learned that one could not fraternize with them—they were there to do her bidding. As a result, the Countess had grown up rather lonely, living in an out-of-the way place with just her mother and father for company, the latter being away much of the time anyway, pursuing his business interests in Alaska and Canada. While she did receive instruction from various tutors, she never had school chums and the like.

Her mother's goal in life was to make the Countess marriageable and she had certainly succeeded. Her father's business interests brought him into contact with other wealthy individuals who had sons for him to consider as a suitable match. Some even had titles. So the Countess received her title, marrying a German Count whose father had made business inroads in the logging industry in Alaska, and the marriage had actually been relatively happy. Her husband had a passing knowledge of Russian and they both were relatively proficient in English, so communication between them was not too difficult. His death and the death of her only child had been catastrophic, but over time, she had learned to accept the loss. But again, more loneliness.

She sighed and looked across the table at her companion, noticing the girl staring at her, while the waiter cleared his throat to get her attention, and realized that she had yet to study the menu. Roused from her reverie, the Countess resumed her *modus operandi.* "Waiter, a glass of red wine and be quick about it!"

Annie Lee studied her employer across the table, seeing her drop into her evening funk. Being used to her long silences, Annie knew that the Countess was in her own little world right now.

Just once I wish that she would ask me how I'm doing, instead of barking orders, she thought sourly. Her name wasn't even "Annie," that was just what the Countess called her. Her real name was An Lee, or at least it was until her parents gave her away to the Countess to be trained as her maid. *I know she mourns the loss of her husband and her son, but I haven't had the chance to marry or bear a child. I'm just an appendage to this woman.*

An clearly remembered the day of her first meeting with the Countess, who apparently had traveled to her village for the express purpose of removing her from her family. Looking up at this tall, middle-aged white woman with a strange accent, she was terrified, clinging to her mother while her father wrested her away and gave her to another Chinese woman accompanying the Countess. She never saw her parents again. Her life had consisted of following the older Chinese woman, Jiaying Zhang, around the various houses occupied by the Countess, learning housekeeping skills and a smattering of Russian and English, which was sufficient for her purpose in the Countess' household, but not enough, she feared, to allow her to escape to live on her own.

The Countess sipped at her wine while Annie sucked on the straw in her Diet Coke.

The Countess thought back to her honeymoon years ago, some of it also spent on an ocean liner (albeit a much larger one than this vessel) on the transatlantic journey to Europe. Even to this day, the romance of it made her smile. To be free from her mother's suffocating social routines, to be doted on by her new husband, who always took time to comment on her beautiful long dark hair and firm figure, not appearing to care that her height almost matched his, and to finally feel cosmopolitan, rather than to just read about it. They had traveled by sea to the port of Vancouver, Canada, and then took a train the full length of the country to board a luxury liner bound for Paris. Her father had spared no expense in providing the details of the honeymoon. Accommodation on the train and the liner had been first-class, and the hotels and villas in Europe were classic and luxurious.

The Countess looked around the dining room again, spotting the grey-haired woman who had smiled at her in the elevator earlier. She might be nice to talk to.

An bent over her dinner as she watched the Countess begin to eat. The Countess usually had her eat in the kitchen, which An actually preferred, because she could watch television to improve her English as long as she kept the volume low. Here, she could only look around the room, since the window seats had been taken and the Countess did not appear to care about the view.

Across the room she noticed a relatively young Chinese man walk toward a table for two and wondered about him. Would someone else be joining him? She hoped not, speculating on the chance of meeting him on a walk, perhaps, during one of the Countess' afternoon naps. One thing about age, An mused, was that her employer required more sleep, which meant An could enjoy a little more time on her own. If the man looked over at their table she would smile at him, hoping to get his attention. She wondered if he was a photographer, since he carried a camera on a strap around his neck.

Chapter 9

"I can't believe we're doing this!" Olive exclaimed the next morning as she walked out onto the veranda, reveling in the beautiful blue sky. She shielded her eyes from the light bouncing off the gentle waves as the ship headed north through the Inner Passage on its way to Alaska.

Jean walked out to join her, putting her arm around her shoulder, knowing that Olive's thoughts had turned to Howard. "Make sure you get lots of photos—like this one, for instance," she said, showing one she had taken earlier while Olive was in the bathroom. "Tell you what, Maggie's in the bathroom now and you're still in your robe, so I'm going to grab the elevator and scope out the buffet at the Lido, or whatever it's called, to see if there are tables available for breakfast."

Jean arrived on the Lido deck to a din of humanity, with a number of children also in attendance. The line at the omelette station was long, although moving efficiently, but all of the window seats were taken. After grabbing a plate and piling it with fruit and pastries, she took the elevator back to the suite, knowing that there was a coffee maker waiting. Rather than deal with the crowd, she figured the fruit and pastries could hold them until they either went to an early lunch back at the buffet or enjoyed a burger by the pool.

As Jean walked through the door, Maggie exited the bathroom. "Well, what do we have here? Room service? I was hoping for someone better-looking!"

Jean just stuck out her tongue and put the plate on the table in the sitting room. "Why don't you make yourself useful, Maggie, and put some water in the coffee maker."

Olive giggled, seeing them up to their old antics. "Well, you can take the girls out of New York . . ." she chuckled.

Jean walked toward the veranda. "While I'm really looking forward to the shore excursions, today will be so relaxing—just hanging around the ship, maybe doing some pool time this afternoon. Apparently, there's a good chance of seeing a whale or two. And tonight there's a musical production in the theater. The shows are supposed to be really professional."

Maggie turned on the television. "This is cool," she cried. "The ship posts onboard activities for the day."

Olive joined her to look at the activity program. "Look here!" she exclaimed. "Someone who knows about gold mining in the Yukon is giving a short lecture in the library area at noon. I think I'll see what that's about. It won't cut into relaxation time, either, if you two are interested."

Jean and Maggie just shook their heads.

Turning her thoughts toward other activities, Olive moved on. "I'm conflicted about whether to join the two couples tonight for dinner," she admitted. "Jack made quite a scene last night, but on the other hand, once his food came, he was too busy to talk, so the conversation with Karen and Art was interesting. I didn't realize they both have health issues, but Art says that with medication, his heart condition is under control and the required exercise, I guess, is a benefit for him."

Maggie nodded. "Poor Karen, though. You'd expect a little support from your spouse, but Jack was treating her like a hypochondriac or something. Like she was faking. I've read that you can die if you don't have an EpiPen handy to counteract whatever causes the problem, because you actually can't breathe. That would be terrifying! And yet she didn't make a big deal about it. She just asked the server about a couple of ingredients."

The women took their cups of coffee and the plate of food out to the veranda. Olive mused silently, looking back on last evening. Art and Karen had gone with the women to the quiz at the pub and had a great time, as it was a really boisterous crowd—a lot of Australians, including Arnie and Alice, although they both appeared to still be somewhat under the weather. Alice looked particularly flushed, but she was a nurse, after all, so Olive had kept her thoughts to herself. There was much laughter from the audience, as the quizmaster was really quite funny; he also doubled as the acoustic guitarist after the quiz, which was a pleasant surprise. Jack and Bev had opted for the casino instead, reducing the air pressure around the table appreciably.

Maggie wiped a croissant crumb off her lap. "I don't mind trying another dinner at their table," she said. "If we sit like we did last night, we can hopefully ignore Jack. He and Bev only seem to talk golf between themselves anyway."

Suddenly they heard an announcement from the captain over the loudspeakers. "Folks, look out your starboard side to see a family of whales!"

Just at that moment, Olive spied a whale breaching, coming right out of the water and splashing back down, within easy sighting distance from the ship, and rushed to get her camera. Trailing behind the larger whale was a pod of three or more smaller whales.

"Holy moly!" Jean exclaimed. "This is fantastic! I've seen this sort of thing on TV, but this is real. I'm glad we're on the right side of the ship."

The whales continued on, keeping abreast of the ship for a while. Since the Inner Passage kept them moderately close to land, the women were also able to sight a couple of eagles and saw some seals frolicking closer to shore.

"I wonder if Jack or Bev will even bother to check out these creatures?" Jean scoffed. While sitting with Art and Karen during the quiz, they had learned that each couple occupied a smaller suite on the same deck as the women. Jean continued, "I'm sure both Art and Karen would be fascinated, but unless the seals are swinging golf clubs, I don't imagine their spouses will find them interesting."

Later in the morning, the women made their way to the pool area. It appeared that a number of people had chosen to whale watch on the outer decks, leaving the pool area less crowded.

"Having that veranda to ourselves is a godsend," Maggie said with a grin. "We don't have to stand out on the deck to see stuff, so we almost have the pool to ourselves! And while that pastry was nice, I think I'm going to get a slice of pizza to eat while I read."

Chapter 10

Olive entered the library area just before noon,
curious whether other passengers shared her interest in
the gold mining days which had made the Yukon area
famous. She spotted a man in a cardigan sweater,
slacks, and loafers setting up a slide projector in front
of a few seats. Olive introduced herself to the fellow—
his name was Bob—who told her he was a retired
geologist and couldn't pass up a chance to share his
knowledge, even though the purpose of this trip was to
celebrate his fortieth anniversary, but since his wife
shared in his passion for the Yukon, taking time out of
his day for this presentation wasn't a problem.

Olive internally grimaced on two accounts. She felt
sure that Howard would have really enjoyed this
presentation, and also wondered if Art had seen the
notice on the television. Surely this would be right up
his alley. Realizing she wouldn't have time to alert him,
she just took a seat.

As she sat down she heard other voices, as two
groups of people walked toward Bob. Behind them she
spotted the Countess, of all people, so she motioned to
her and pointed at an adjacent chair. In return, the
Countess gave a slight wave, and, resplendent in a
tartan skirt and cashmere sweater, topped with a
luxuriant braid of bright black hair (Mother Nature had
no part in that!), she strode toward Olive.

Just after the hour, Bob announced that he would
begin, as twelve passengers had already joined him.
After giving the group a little of his professional

background, he launched into his slide presentation. "Just a warning," he said. "I don't plan on getting into the history of the train from Skagway to the Summit, as you will receive lots of information about the travel woes of the miners on their way to fame and fortune if you take the shore excursion out of Skagway. The scenery is breathtaking and the narration is very informative; I highly recommend it. I've been on the train before and it's amazing."

Olive nodded, knowing that the excursion was definitely on their list of things to do in Skagway. She heard the Countess mutter something next to her, but couldn't make out what she was saying. There was a general murmur in the audience as they waited expectantly for the presentation to begin in earnest.

Bob didn't disappoint. "Gold has held an allure for a lot of folks for a lot of years, and as history witnessed in the mid-eighteen-hundreds in California, men would leave behind families and employment to search for it, dreaming of panning huge nuggets which would make them millionaires. In bad economic times, the chance of striking it rich caused some to risk everything they had, including their lives, to join the throng. Some three hundred thousand hopefuls were part of that gold rush.

"Decades later, just before the turn of the twentieth century—in 1896, to be exact—a couple of prospectors in the Yukon *did* strike it rich, setting off a three-year stampede, where over one hundred thousand prospective miners tried to follow suit. While some gold had been found in 1870 in southern Alaska, the excitement surrounding the rush to the Klondike area, in what is now near Dawson City, the Yukon, in northern Canada, was reminiscent of the wild, wild California days. As a side note, the name 'Klondike' is actually a mispronunciation of the native word 'Tr'ondëk,' meaning 'part of a river.'"

Olive looked around at the other participants, who were clearly finding Bob's information just as interesting as she was.

Bob moved on to slides showing men bending down by creeks, holding pick axes and pans. "As you can see, the work was hard, wet, and often cold. The men were trying to dig away rocks from the creek shores, while also looking into the water itself for any glint of gold flakes stuck in the hard soil—or better yet, actual gold nuggets. They would put their pans into the water and then sift the pans back and forth in hopes of finding chunks large enough to keep. Then rinse and repeat, so to speak." This brought a chuckle from the group.

Bob continued. "As you can see from this slide, the miners erected simple tents, which were part of the goods and food that the Yukon authorities made them bring—or else they were turned back. Many of the gold rush crowd were true tenderfoots, coming from cities with a hope and a dream and little else, so the authorities were trying to prevent the miners from killing themselves trying to get rich quick. But you'll learn more about that on the train excursion.

"Panning for gold is also called 'placer mining.' Even today you are allowed to stake a claim, if it hasn't already been staked. And it can still be done the old-fashioned way—by placing a stake at the four corners of the claim. Staking the claim doesn't give you ownership of the land, just whatever gold you are able to extract. While some people still go to the Yukon in summers to try to pan for gold the old-fashioned way, even the smaller operations now employ sluices to run silt and water through them to separate any gold particles which might be present in the silt. As the price of gold goes up and down, profitability is also affected."

At this point, Olive was startled to hear the Countess speak up in her heavily accented English. "Not that it would affect anyone here, but if you own the land in which the creek lies," she said, "you can live there—build a cabin, for instance—and search for gold in the summers."

Bob viewed the Countess with interest. "That sounds like an adventurous way to live!" he exclaimed.

The Countess replied in a soft voice, "An adventurous way to die, maybe . . ."

Olive heard the exchange and was shocked. What did the Countess mean?

Bob had obviously heard too, and he looked quizzically at the Countess, but chose not to pursue the matter. "People ask me if I have ever found any gold, and I can report that, yes, I have, although I'm glad I kept my day job," he said, carrying on with the presentation. "My wife and I have camped out for a month a couple of times in the summer, but we're too old for that now. Good memories, though. If you have any questions, now is the time to ask." And the presentation was over.

The Countess began to rise, so Olive decided to walk with her, wanting so much to get a little background on her sad exchange with Bob. The Countess' eyes were a little teary, so Olive put a hand on her shoulder, hoping to start a conversation.

"Thank you for your concern," the Countess acknowledged Olive. "It was a long time ago, but it still grieves me. Perhaps at some later time we can discuss it. It might be good for me to tell someone. You look like a caring person." With that, the Countess moved more quickly ahead, so Olive headed back to the suite.

Chapter 11

The afternoon by the pool passed by leisurely, just as
the women had hoped. Had Art or Karen joined them, it
would have been alright, but not having either of the
couples to converse with was a bit of a relief. Olive had
reported on Bob's presentation in the library, including
the Countess' odd reaction.

Maggie shrugged. "It certainly sounds like she's
carrying a lot of baggage. I wonder what happened."

By four o'clock, though, Jean was getting restless.
"I'd like to sit on the veranda, watch the world go by
and enjoy a beverage before dinner," she announced.

As one, the women all rose from their seats at the
suggestion. There was ample time to shower and get
ready for the gala dinner that evening.

Again, Olive went through the entrance of the dining
room and spotted Karen waving them over to their
table. Maggie and Jean followed, also in their new long
dress skirts and blouses, feeling a little self-conscious,
but good about themselves, too.

"You all look lovely!" Art commented.

Bev opened her mouth. "Yeah, and I'm chopped
liver?" she snapped.

Art sat back, telling Bev that he had already
complimented her, and, in fact, had gifted her with the
new necklace she was wearing.

While Olive commented that it was beautiful, Jack
just smirked. Karen sat quietly, her eyes skyward. Yet
another moment of awkward silence followed.

Olive surveyed the room, as she had the previous night. This time, there were some tuxedoes and long gowns to be seen—indeed, Jack was resplendent in a tuxedo, while Art sported a nice suit.

Olive thought back to Bill, who had worn a rented tuxedo at Jon's wedding, but couldn't wait to "get out of the monkey suit." Howard looked good in a suit, too, but she doubted whether fancy dress was his style. She would ask him when she returned to New York; she didn't find dressing up to be all that bad.

It being a gala dinner meant even more glorious food. Olive ordered the foie gras as a starter, reading how it was fried then served with a pear half poached in port wine. Even Maggie and Jean were game to try it. The featured entrée was prime rib with lobster tail, which everyone at the table chose.

Jean grinned from ear to ear. "A true carnivore's delight!"

Jack, not to be outdone, ordered two ribs and lobster tails. Olive murmured to Jean, "Well, at least it will keep him quiet," to which Jean snorted, "Let's hope Holland America doesn't go broke on his meal choices."

Art asked the women if they planned to do the quiz again and looked a little distressed upon learning that they planned to take in the musical in the theater.

Jack piped up, "There's a show? I wouldn't mind seeing that!"

Karen had not been consulted but looked happy to go, so the two couples agreed to meet at eight o'clock outside the theater. Maggie spoke for the women, telling Jack that the trio would go separately, as it might be difficult to get that many seats together.

Olive was relieved that Maggie had spoken up. They could just go back to their suite and look at the scenery from the veranda without having to consider the couples' plans.

The dinner was filling and delicious, so dessert was not an issue. Though Jean, ever resourceful, asked the server if dessert could be available later through room service, and sighed meaningfully when he told her it would.

Chapter 12

The next afternoon, An had finally found herself enjoying the trip, free of the Countess and away from the ship for at least a couple of hours. When her employer had the short seminar on Yukon gold mining the day before, she hadn't invited An along—nor did An want to go along.

During that time, she had been able to walk along the promenade like other passengers, pretending to view the Inside Passage and "ooh" and "aah" at the whales, while really trying to discreetly locate the one other Chinese person on the ship, the man with the camera. But she had to keep track of her time, as the Countess would expect to find her back in their suite after the seminar.

An's patience was rewarded when she spotted the man leaning against the railing some ways ahead of her, staring thoughtfully at the scenery. She had an Alaskan guidebook from the cruise company, so she decided on a straightforward approach.

Arriving at his spot, she cleared her throat and addressed him in Mandarin. "Excuse me, do you read English?" She held out her guidebook and pointed to the page regarding the helicopter excursion.

Looking a little startled—but interested—the man responded in Mandarin. "Yes, I do speak and understand English, as I live in Vancouver, but my Mandarin is not all that good," he admitted. "I speak it with my grandmother to practice." He took the guidebook and spoke in a mixture of English and Mandarin, describing the time of departure for the helicopter and the glacier it would visit.

An knew she should have thought through her plan a little better, because she also spoke and read enough English to understand the guidebook, but she wanted to keep up the pretense. In mixed Mandarin and English, she said, "I read it through many times, but was not sure of the information. I want to ask my employer if I can go on the trip to see the ice."

The man smiled, perhaps suspecting her ruse—but maybe not wanting to discourage her, he replied, "I won't be going on the helicopter, but when you return, perhaps you can describe the experience to me over tea. Do you have a cell phone number so we can meet up later?"

After exchanging numbers, they parted, as An had to return to the Countess' suite. Before An left, the man, who had introduced himself as Li-Liang, gave her his cabin number, too.

An bounced down the hallway on her return to the Countess' suite, and had just arrived and taken off her sweater when she heard her employer enter and curtly tell her what to order from room service for a late lunch.

An Lee smiled as the bus drove up to the helicopter terminal. This was going to be an adventure!

The Countess thought herself so clever and of "Annie" as just a simple peasant girl. Ha! An had learned over the years how to protect herself, to the extent that it was possible, by trying to build some savings in case the Countess tossed her aside. She wasn't ready to strike out on her own until she had enough saved, and she resented her employer's hold over her, but unbeknownst to the Countess, she had been skimming off the household money for a few years. She had learned this from the elderly Jiaying, who had been one of the previous maids. An also found that the Countess appeared to have developed enough trust in her to allow the use of a credit card for bigger home expenses—larger outdoor projects, for instance.

An received a household allowance and the Countess rarely checked on it, and especially as she aged, her employer had begun leaving money about, usually in books or coat pockets—not in amounts large enough to set An free, but not enough to be noticed either.

An wanted to go on this helicopter excursion but was certainly not going to use any of her precious cash to fund it, so when she took the credit card to the travel agent to pay for the cruise, she added in one ticket for the excursion. The Countess had been angry when she read the invoice, but An pretended that she thought the Countess intended to go on the flight.

"Stupid girl!" Her employer could rant but do nothing in the way of a refund, so now An happily put on the required foot gear and climbed into helicopter.

An felt such a rush when the helicopter lifted; she was almost a little giddy. To feel the ground falling below her was nothing like she had ever experienced. There were other people in the seats around her, but they must have been strangers, too, because there had been no conversation among them when they put on their special boots, either. In a way, she liked that because she didn't feel excluded—she was just another stranger trying something new.

When the glacier appeared, she was awestruck. Having gone from her childhood home in northern China (a rather barren existence) to the Countess's home in Vancouver had been quite a change—from cold and blustery to warm and almost tropical on some days. Now, stepping onto the glacier, she shuddered.

This was *really* cold!

Grateful for her jacket and gloves, she stepped gingerly, looking down at the blue color under the ice. Luckily, she carried a small camera herself so she could record the moment and show it to her new friend, Li-Liang. The thought made her feel some welcome warmth.

Chapter 13

The Countess paced back and forth in her suite, chagrined that the maid was off on her helicopter adventure. On the one hand, she told herself that she shouldn't begrudge the girl some excitement in her life, but the way it came about bothered the Countess. Perhaps she had been underestimating the girl's cunning. She decided to follow up with the household accounts when they returned to Vancouver, making sure that everything was in order and that no other financial matters were amiss.

She felt restless and lonely. Although Annie was her servant and little conversation passed between them except for the giving and receiving of orders, at least Annie was *there*. Right now, the Countess just had the four walls of her suite to stare at. Looking out to sea really didn't help, either, as the port of Juneau wasn't much different from any other port of call.

Her thoughts took her back to the presentation by that fellow in the library yesterday. She should not have attended, as it only drudged up the memories she was always trying to avoid. Her late husband, Heinz, had shared Bob's passion for the Yukon, a passion which she never really completely understood. While her husband had been attentive to the business his father had started, he also knew that her inherited wealth gave him the freedom to pan for gold during the summers, and, like so many others, he had hoped to make a big strike.

The Countess was willing to let him follow his

dreams, to a certain extent, and even came with him to the Yukon occasionally, traveling via Whitehorse to the Dawson City area, up to the land Heinz had purchased many years before. Early on, he and his younger brother had built a cabin on the property, and although it was very rudimentary, it did have at least a wood stove for warmth. However, the Countess was content to remain in Vancouver for the most part, particularly following the birth of their son, Wilhelm. He had been a miracle baby, really, after so many miscarriages, some late term, making her fear that she would never be a mother.

Little Willie worshipped her husband, and it was only a matter of time before Heinz insisted she bring him to the cabin for at least a couple of weeks during the summer. Heinz had even bought him a little "pan" so he could try his hand at panning for gold. As he grew older, Willie began to share his father's passion for gold, asking to go with him for the full summer season, sharing in his love of the outdoors and learning to hunt like a real prospector. Because Heinz' younger brother had to come and go more often, Willie became a useful partner to his father over time. They were able to find enough gold to justify their effort, and the Countess knew that their lifestyle did not depend on that revenue in any event. In any case, she looked forward to the end of summer each year when both her husband and her son returned to her.

She shook herself, not wanting to go any further in remembering the past. Perhaps she should speak to that nice woman, Olive. It might give her some respite to share her grief with someone willing to listen. At that moment, she heard the lock turning, so she straightened herself and dried her eyes, preparing to give Annie a proper chastisement.

Chapter 14

After An departed the return bus to the ship, she practically ran up the gangplank, hoping to locate Li-Liang right away. She didn't have much time, as she knew the Countess would expect her to report promptly for duty after the excursion.

An decided to detour from her route to the suite to check out the Lido deck in case Li-Liang was there. Sure enough, there he sat, looking lost in thought over a cup of tea.

He glanced up at her approach and his attitude brightened immediately. "Well, did you get to fly the helicopter?" he asked, grinning broadly.

"No. Very lucky. There was a pilot." An was glad that she could just try to speak in her broken English, having decided to give up the pretense of knowing less of it that she did; this would be good practice for when she finally split from the Countess, although it was helpful in some instances to be able to express herself in her native language to Li-Liang.

An took out her small digital camera to show him the landscape, the odd animals spotted en route, and the majesty of the glacier itself, while trying her best in English to describe the whole experience. Li-Liang couldn't help but notice her exuberance, musing that, as a maid, she probably had little time off.

He ordered her a cup of tea and then settled back in his chair. An Lee was an attractive woman, although perhaps not as young as he first thought. He ruefully thought of the description he'd heard from a white man that Chinese women never age—until they get old.

Once her tea arrived, An sighed.

In response, Li-Liang asked if she was alright.

"Yes, I guess. After my tea I should hurry to my employer," she murmured. "It would be nice to just sit here with you. But I am also 'on duty.' I can only rest here for a few minutes."

Li-Liang admired her spontaneity and apparent lack of guile—it was clear from her gestures that she wanted to be with him. *Nothing coy about this one,* he thought.

For An, it was incredible that she was sitting here with a nice Chinese man, probably somewhat older than her, in a restaurant aboard a ship in Alaska. Her parents, assuming they were still alive, would be astounded.

Li-Liang was curious. "I heard the Countess speaking to another woman yesterday and she spoke with an accent. Russian, perhaps? Do you live with her there?" he asked.

An grimaced. "The maid who began my training told me that the Countess was born in eastern Russia. When she married a German Count, they moved to Vancouver because he had business in Alaska and Canada. When she took me from my village in northern China, we just went straight to her home in Vancouver. I never met her husband."

"She *took* you?" Li-Liang, having lived most of his life in Vancouver, couldn't imagine that such practices still existed.

"Jiaying, the older maid, told me that she had also been 'adopted,'" An said, noticing Li-Liang's surprised expression. She switched to Mandarin to explain. "The local authorities in China accepted bribes to provide documents to the Countess in bringing children into Canada. This was quite a while ago, though. And the Countess eventually made me a Canadian somehow, so it's not like I have to go back there if I leave her."

Then Li-Liang asked more questions about the Countess, many more than those he asked of An herself, but she was happy to answer them. She was happy just to be sitting there with him. He seemed to listen caringly while she was describing her unhappiness, what with her separation from her family and having to endure the suffocating life of a maid.

Looking at her watch, An got up to go. Li-Liang assured her that they would see each other again.

Chapter 15

As the ship docked smoothly at seven o'clock in the morning, Maggie greeted their room service delivery with enthusiasm. The young steward rolled in the cart and placed the items they'd ordered on the table in the sitting room. The women had decided to eat an earlier breakfast and then attend to their grooming.

Since the ship was in port until nine o'clock that evening, they had plenty of time to take the mid-morning train ride toward the Yukon in Canada, enjoy a light lunch back on ship, and then return to shore for a streetcar tour of the area.

Later, they were just ready to leave when they heard a tentative knock on the door.

Olive opened it to a smiling Karen.

"This should be such fun!" she exclaimed.

Behind her, Olive could see Jack and the others striding by. Not being sure that he would hold the elevator for them, Karen and the three ladies moved quickly to catch up.

"Here you go, Art!" Jack bellowed as they walked into the elevator. "The kitchen gave Bev and me sandwiches and juice, so we got one for you, too," he said, quickly spinning Art around and putting the small sack in his backpack.

"I'm not sure I'll need it, but thanks," Art said, somewhat flustered. "The hike is supposed to take four to five hours, so I'll see all of you later in the day."

The group moved toward the gangplank, pulling out their identification cards along the way. Karen dropped back to walk with Olive, while Jack and Bev strode along in front. Jack stuffed his golf glove, while Art carried a waterproof windbreaker strapped to his small backpack, and sported hiking boots and thick socks. The day did not portend rain, but while Olive and her group would be undercover on the train, he would be exposed to the elements for a number of hours.

"This is so cool!" Jean exclaimed as the women walked up to the train station. Handing their tickets to the "conductor" they were able to board one of the cars. "Hmm, the Skagway White Pass and Yukon Railway," she read aloud from a sign. "That's quite a handle."

Just as Olive got herself settled in a seat across from Maggie and Jean and next to Karen, she saw the Countess boarding their car, so she beckoned the older woman to sit next to her. While she watched the guide walk toward her microphone at the front, Olive turned to Maggie, Jean, and Karen and introduced them to the Countess, who smiled graciously and turned back to face the front of the car.

The round trip was to last between three and four hours; they would travel to a site very near the Yukon border and then return to the ship. Along the way, they would be treated to awe-inspiring gorges, waterfalls, and steep rock cliffs, sometimes covered with wire mesh to deal with possible landslides.

The conductor began the ride by telling them that, in 1896, three prospectors had found flakes of gold in Bonanza Creek in the Klondike area of the Yukon. When the word got out, it created a frenzy similar to the one in California and the Canadian gold rush was on.

Hopefuls came from all over the world, particularly from the U.S., which was in the midst of a depression. Everyone was trying to strike it rich, with many prospectors having no clue about the dangers which lay ahead. They had to cross six hundred miles of steep hikes and waterways just to reach the gold fields. Some tried the shorter route along the incredibly steep Chilkoot trail, while others chose the longer, safer White Pass Trail. Since officials forced them to have at least one ton of supplies, both routes resulted in the deaths of both men and pack animals. A local businessman had tried to build a road along the first part of the journey, but that plan didn't work out, so some investors hit upon the plan for a narrow-gauge railway to take the prospectors through the most dangerous part of the route.

The railway was completed in 1898 and, as the conductor explained, the building of it was a story in itself, involving thousands of men and tons of dynamite. The daring builder, "Big Mike" Henry, was quoted as saying, "Give me enough dynamite and snooze and I'll build you a railway to hell!" He laid over a hundred miles of track. Olive cringed just thinking about the hardship.

After the gold rush ended, the train was still in use for a number of years; then it lay dormant until it was reintroduced as a tourist attraction to boost the sagging fortunes of Skagway. Now the train's green and yellow engines and the picturesque passenger cars traveled in and out of the town with regularity.

In the higher elevation there was some rain, but the passengers were able to get a good look at the advertised gorges, long trestles, and waterfalls while listening to the fascinating narrative. The ride was a forty-mile round trip, going from sea level to the White Pass Summit—at 2,865 feet above sea level—and back again.

At the summit, while the passengers were waiting for the ride back down to Skagway, Olive took the opportunity to speak to the Countess. "Yesterday at the presentation you appeared to know a lot about the Klondike?" she asked.

The Countess nodded grimly. "I must apologize for my comments. It was not my intention to distract from Bob's narration. I am afraid that my thoughts had drifted to the past, causing me to blurt out something better left unsaid."

Olive patted her arm. "Countess, if you are grieving, for any reason, it is sometimes best to share it. It does lift a load. When my husband died suddenly three years ago, I thought my life would end, but thankfully, having friends and family to talk to allowed me to share my grief, and while I still miss him, going on with my life has been my salvation," she said. "Do you mind me asking what happened?"

The Countess appeared to consider the question. "Even though it happened a long time ago, it is still hard to talk about, because it was not only my husband who perished, but my teenage son as well."

Olive gasped, trying to imagine the horror of that experience. She didn't know what she would do if she lost Jon. "Please, go on."

"My late husband was obsessed with finding gold," the Countess started. "He did not need the money; we were doing well in business and I had a substantial inheritance from my parents. He had bought acreage in the Klondike area many, many years ago, through which there ran a creek, and he had staked a number of claims so that he and his younger brother could work on them during the summers. He had even built a cabin on the land, rather than using a tent. At the end of every summer, he would bring home enough gold to fuel his 'fever,' so to speak, so there was no way of dissuading him. He and his brother also enjoyed hunting and fishing—the real outdoor life—so they were able to augment the canned food, flour, coffee and the like that they brought with them.

"I was tolerant of his absence and even joined him at some point each summer, but panning for gold and hunting and fishing were not my passions, so it was not only boring but uncomfortable for me, especially when mosquitoes were at their worst. When I finally gave birth to our son, Willie, I stopped going altogether. The first summer after Willie was born Heinz stayed home, but the next year saw him back on the property. He was so attentive to Willie during the other months of the year that I couldn't complain.

"Eventually, even though Willie was still a young child, Heinz asked me to bring our son for at least part of the season, so I would visit a few weeks during his school holidays, until Willie was ten years old."

Olive pursed her lips. *This next part can't be good,* she thought.

The Countess wiped her eyes and continued. "At that point, Willie demanded to accompany his father for the full summer. He adored his father so! I had enrolled him over the years in summer activities in Vancouver, but by then he had rejected them, wishing probably for more 'authentic' activities provided by the Klondike. Heinz had begun teaching him how to shoot, which I hated, but once he saw his father bring down a deer, he too wanted to provide their dinner, as he put it."

The train was now traveling the track back to Skagway and the Countess told Olive, in her heavily accented English, that she didn't want to interrupt her sightseeing to hear an old woman weep.

Olive immediately responded, "Oh, I took many photos on the way up and was able to view much of the scenery we're passing now, so please go on!"

The Countess looked over at her gratefully. "It was in my son's sixteenth year that my husband and he were hunting about two miles from the cabin. I only know what I've been told, but apparently Heinz' brother stayed behind at the cabin because he wasn't feeling well. They had all planned to take a day off from the search for gold anyway, so the hunting trip probably made sense. Late in the day, my brother-in-law realized something was wrong, because neither Heinz nor Willie had returned to the cabin."

When the Countess began to sniffle, Olive waited for her to continue. "After a search around the cabin area, my brother-in-law set out, going further up the creek, which was at some points quite deep and still had some movement in it from unexpected summer rains," the Countess said shakily. "About a mile upriver, he spotted what he thought was a body, and then another one. Rushing toward them, he stepped gingerly into the water, not wanting to lose his balance. Since it was at a bend in the creek, the bodies had become snagged on some rocks and foliage, allowing him to grab each body in turn and drag them onto the bank."

Olive watched the Countess begin weeping fully, drawing attention from some of the other passengers, so Olive moved toward her, trying to shield her from prying eyes.

The Countess appeared determined to finish her narrative once her sobbing abated. "My brother-in-law turned each body over, trying to determine each cause of death. He told me later that he looked at my son first, and there appeared to be no sign of injury. But in examining Heinz, he found a large bullet wound in his chest, probably from one of their hunting rifles. Back at the cabin, he had a short wave radio he could use to call authorities, but he didn't want to leave the bodies overnight for local predators to mangle. Knowing that the creek carried downstream next to the cabin, he told me he decided to use mother nature to help him get

Heinz and Willie out of the open. He maneuvered them back into the creek, toward the middle, and then pushed them forward, being careful of his footing.

"Arriving at the cabin, he pulled them up onto the bank, made his short wave contact with Dawson City and then dragged Willie and Heinz into the cabin for safekeeping. A helicopter brought stretchers and a mounted police officer, who at first was critical of the bodies being moved, because the fellow clearly was not aware of the wilderness, but he did agree to accompany my brother-in-law to search for the rifles."

The train was nearing Skagway, but Olive encouraged the Countess to complete her thoughts.

"They did find the two rifles and were able to load them onto the helicopter," the Countess said. "My brother-in-law was allowed to close up the cabin and accompany Heinz and Willie to Dawson City, so that he could call me. It was the middle of the night by the time I received his call, a call that no one can prepare for. I was hysterical and only had an older Chinese maid there to help. She was able to bring me some brandy and to call my physician to attend, as she was concerned I might have a stroke or something. It was just terrible! The next week or so, getting them back and burying them were the hardest days of my life. I cannot forget that."

Olive had a question, but wondered whether to ask it. Thinking it might give the Countess closure, she ventured. "Did the police determine your son's cause of death?"

"Yes. The Mounties figured that my son must have accidentally shot my husband—the wounds were from his rifle, as the bullet had lodged in Heinz' body—and when his body fell into the creek, Willie must have jumped in after him, and drowned trying to move his father toward the shore. I am so sad about losing my husband, but I'm really angry with him, too, for letting Willie hunt. I also feel guilty for not putting up more of a protest."

Sharing her story appeared to have calmed the Countess, and she hugged Olive in thanks for her attentiveness. She dried her tears and said to all three women, "Do not let my weeping affect the rest of your day. I am going to my suite to rest, but I will surely see you later."

Alighting from the train, Olive was happy that she had been able to help the Countess in some small way. She was also happy to pay twenty dollars for a video and commemorative hat for Howard. Looking over at Maggie and Jean, she told them, "We'll have to cook you both some steak and pretend it's a moose or something, and then show the video to Howard!"

Jean smiled. "I'll wear a plaid shirt."

Chapter 16

Art began his walk up the trail, breathing in the clear, cool air. The scent of pine was wonderful—this was so different from the trails near home. Having enjoyed a hearty room service breakfast and done some stretching exercises while Bev was showering, he felt fit and ready for a day in the open.

Hearing some giggling, he turned to see four young women loping up the trail behind him. One of them called out for him to wait.

He was gratified to see that they were puffing a little when they arrived, so he teased them: "I thought it was only old fogies like me who got winded trying to run uphill!"

One of the girls introduced herself and her companions; her name was Jill. "Actually, we're cross country runners, if you can believe it, but we didn't do any warm-ups before trying to race up this path, so we're ready just to stroll now along with you, if you'd be okay with that."

Art grinned. "What man wouldn't want to be accompanied by a bevy of beauties on this wonderful day!"

As they continued up the trail, Jill informed him that they were starting to train for the college team season. They planned to go as far as Sturgil's Landing, have lunch, and then branch off onto another trail before returning to Skagway. He told them that he planned to turn back at Sturgil's Landing so that he could be back at the cruise ship in time, hopefully, to join friends who were going on a bus tour of the area.

"Oh, you're a tourist, then? Where are you from?" Jill asked.

When Art said New York, the girls all squealed.

"Oh, I'd love to go there!" one exclaimed. "What's it like to live in the Big Apple?"

Art told them he lived in Westchester County, just outside of Manhattan, and wouldn't live in Manhattan on a dare, preferring the relative peace and quiet of his home area. The young women did not see how he could feel that way, saying that they wanted to get away from Alaska and see the world. Art just chuckled.

After a good walk, the party spotted water in the distance and soon came upon a creek with a picnic table and a bathroom station. The young women plunked themselves down and started hauling out bags of sandwiches and apples.

Jill motioned for Art to join them. "We've brought way too much food and we don't want to keep carrying it, so please, join us."

The view of the remains of a sawmill across the creek provided a nice backdrop to the picnic, and Art appreciated the time to rest before he had to move again. The half-hour respite would serve him well on the way down.

Art said goodbye to the group as they were putting on their packs and began his return walk to the ship. The hike up the trail had been strenuous, but invigorating, too. It had been listed as a "moderate" hike, four to five hours in duration—just perfect! He had not seen any bears, nor did he want to. Being close to nature was one thing, but this city boy didn't wish to get up close and personal with anything that might attack him! Although having a somewhat noisy party of

women with him had no doubt scared away most
creatures.

The view on the way up the trail had been
breathtaking against the blue sky, the forest on display,
with stands of spruce, hemlock, and pine all around. He
had been sweating a little bit in the warmth, but the
footing was overall pretty good.

As he strolled back, Art wished his son, Matt, was
beside him. They would both have walked quietly,
looking over the town of Skagway and the harbor,
enjoying the view and each other's company. While he
had enjoyed the young group's company, he had hiked
many times alone, and so far the medicine was doing its
job for his heart, so safety wasn't an issue with him.
The solitude did, however, lend itself to brooding,
something he preferred to avoid.

His marriage had never been a happy one and
wouldn't have happened but for Bev's pregKaren when
Art was finishing college. Bev always blamed him for
it, as though she had nothing to do with it, always
reminding Art of all the things she could have done . . .
and hearing her gripe about him being "just a
schoolteacher" while praising Jack to the hilt for his
insurance business; that really got on Art's nerves, too.
But Bev had been a good mother to Matt and had been
easier to live with once Matt was older and she'd gone
back to school to complete her business degree, leading
to her job selling investment products.

Art had decided to retire when he could receive full
benefits, and Bev worked part-time setting up 401K
retirement plans for small businessmen. But even
though Art had a good pension and had earned his
retirement, Bev liked to tell anyone who would listen
that she was the breadwinner and all he did was hike all
day. Art was proud of Bev for her hard work and
ambition, building up her business, and often told her

how proud he was. But it seemed that the more successful she became, the poorer her memory became regarding his contributions over the years to their comfortable lifestyle now.

He sometimes wondered about Bev and Jack. She had met Jack a few years ago as part of her business and had participated with him in charity golf tournaments a few times. Jack had convinced them to join the country club so that Bev could golf there, and they seemed to spend a lot of time together. Art had made an effort and went to functions at the club with Bev, but it wasn't his style. Looking over at Karen at those functions, he could see that she, too, was less than enthralled.

A few months ago, Karen had mentioned the idea of a cruise while the couples ate at the club. She was so enthused and had obviously worked on Jack, but when Bev suggested they go along, Art was flabbergasted. She had not mentioned it until it looked like Jack was willing to go. The idea of spending that much time in an enclosed space with Jack had gnawed at him, but he didn't want to be a spoilsport. He couldn't believe it when he heard Bev tell Olive and the other women that she only came on the cruise because of Art. Jeez.

Oh, well, at least out here it was quiet and scenic. Apparently, hiking was not a favorite cruise excursion, so he had been surprised when the young women caught up with him on the trek up.

He stopped to sit on a rock, gazing out over the scenery. Having done some reading before taking the cruise, he thought about this area of the world, and how European explorers had so dramatically changed it. His imagination brought images of early Native people living in small villages, in harmony with nature. It must have been traumatizing for them to look out at the water, seeing sailing ships disgorging rowboats filled with white faces. He chuckled about the tour Karen was taking—a train built specially for gold miners, for God's sake. Imagine the blasting and clearing of trees the rails and trestles would have required. And worse yet, his wife, Bev, and that idiot, Jack, driving around on indigenous land carved out for a golf course!

Art didn't know why, but he began to feel uneasy, although when he looked up and down the trail, he saw no one walking either way. It was like someone was watching him. He shook it off, thinking maybe it was the wind in the trees or the absence of his earlier walking companions—kind of silly, really.

Looking at his watch, he continued down the trail, not wanting to worry anyone, although there was still some of the afternoon left. Maybe if he got back in time, he could join the women on the streetcar tour.

The trail began to slope more steeply toward the end of his hike. *Probably why those young women had been puffing when they tried to run to catch up with me at the outset,* Art thought. He slowed to keep his footing as the wind began to whistle.

Seeing no one come along from the trail's starting point, he stopped for a moment, holding onto a tree branch while looking forward. He caught a shadow from the corner of his eye and then felt a hard push that drove him to the ground.

Before Art could look up, he felt a sharp pain in his neck and some movement around him. He felt a second hard push, this time driving his face onto the trail. He lost consciousness momentarily, and then felt a tug at the identification lanyard around his neck. Then, not being sure of any possible injury, he slowly pushed himself up into a kneeling position, looking around him to see if there were fellow hikers he could call on.

Crawling over to one of the trees, he boosted himself until he stood, shakily wondering what the heck had happened. He started again to walk down the trail, but shortly, his vision began to blur and his gait became unsteady.

Chapter 17

An witnessed the Countess' departure from the train excursion. An had been happy to stay behind, which left her enough time to walk over to the center of town, although she would have to be sure to return in time to meet the train. She had hoped she would run into Li-Liang again, but he must have either stayed on board the ship or taken some other excursion. The notice on the television in their room had also mentioned the availability of hiking trails.

Now back at the train station, An started walking toward the Countess, who appeared to be waiting for her, but then stopped, seeing her employer pause to greet a middle-aged man with whom she must be familiar, because she allowed him to give her a kiss on the cheek. He was nice-looking, with a rather ruddy complexion and a full beard, like someone from the Old West in the television shows. Behind the Countess, An saw the three women who were always together, one of them gesturing excitedly at the hat one of the others was carrying. She saw the woman carrying the hat glance over at the Countess, but the Countess was clearly engrossed in her conversation with the stranger, pointing at the suitcase he was carrying.

An decided to keep walking, assuming that the Countess would acknowledge her and beckon her over. As she got closer, she thought she heard the Countess say, "So you had a good summer? Were you able to sew them into the clothes?"

The man replied, "Yes. I took my share and also

paid expenses, but I think you'll be very happy with this. There were no problems at Customs on the way down from Whitehorse."

At that point, the Countess looked over and spotted An. "Annie. This is a private conversation," she said sharply. "Stand by the ship and I'll call you when I'm ready."

An nodded and turned slowly, still hoping to catch more of the conversation.

She heard the man say, "I've got to take the motor coach tour back to Whitehorse. I'll email you soon about next year."

Moving further away, An was unable to hear anything more, but her mind was racing with possibilities. Maybe the man was just carrying the suitcase on a trip, but the way the Countess had pointed at it made it appear that she was to receive it. Pretending disinterest, An stood by the gangplank, watching passengers file on, including the three women she had noticed before, talking to a fourth woman she didn't recognize.

Finally, she heard the Countess bark her name and tell her "to be quick about it." The man then handed the suitcase to An as the Countess strode toward the ship. She heard him call out "Have a good trip, Auntie!" to which the Countess merely waved over her shoulder.

"Does this woman not love anyone?" An muttered to herself.

Arriving at their suite, the Countess had the maid set the suitcase on her bed. Then she said, "Annie, go down to the buffet area and bring me a pastry and a cup of coffee. I don't feel like using room service."

With Annie out of the room, the Countess took the key her grand-nephew had given her and opened the suitcase. In it were two gowns, old ones that the Countess had mailed to him in Whitehorse. They may have been old, she chuckled to herself, but they were now *very* valuable. She felt around the bodice and hem of each, finding small bumps sewn in. She didn't want to disturb the stitching—she'd do that back in Vancouver—but she could feel the bumps were of different sizes, with some being significantly larger than the others. Just then, she heard the door open, so she quickly closed and locked the suitcase.

An could not help but notice the glow on her employer's face. Was she coming down with something? An hoped not, because the Countess became a true Russian bear when she was ill, even with just a little summer cold, and being stuck in the same room with her would be hell on earth.

But An was surprised to find the Countess almost cheerful, telling her to enjoy the rest of the afternoon off. An decided to press her luck and ask if she could use the pool and order pizza and beer there. To her surprise, the Countess agreed.

After An left for the pool, the Countess decided to enjoy her pastry and coffee before going back to the suitcase. While talking with Olive had been cathartic, it also required more energy than she was used to, so she was hungry. All of what she had told Olive was true, and the tears had been cleansing, in a way, but she would never share with her, or anyone else, the reason for this trip.

Opening up the suitcase, the Countess marveled at the beauty of the gowns, gowns that she had worn to galas and other events on the arm of her husband. She had been beautiful back then, and while Vancouver was not London or Paris by any means, it did have a social season, and she and her husband were in demand at the various functions supporting the arts. Leaving their son with his nanny, they would enjoy the evening, replete with food and cocktails and sometimes music, the Count guiding her around the dance floor. That was all gone now, and had been for years.

Following the death of Heinz and Willie, she never wanted to visit the Klondike again. Her brother-in-law offered to keep the property and placer claims going, as his interest in gold matched her husband's, so she agreed to not sell the property for the time being. He visited her in Vancouver sometimes, bringing along *his* son, who was somewhat younger than Willie would have been, and, like Willie, was also developing an obsession with gold. During these trips, they often brought some gold with them, enough to show her that the property was worth keeping. She thought at first to refuse it, as it usually just brought back bad memories, but she then concluded that the Klondike *owed* her the gold, so she struck a deal, giving her part of the found gold, after payment of expenses, and leaving the other share to her brother-in-law—and his son, if he chose to carry on.

By the early nineties, her brother-in-law noticed that the creek and shoreline had shifted somewhat—perhaps the result of some earthquakes off the coast of Alaska ten to twenty years before. He asked the Countess to travel to the site in order to discuss the future of the endeavor. When she arrived, her grand-nephew, who was doing much of the work by then, presented her with a rather large nugget, telling her that there was more where that came from, or at least so he believed.

They had a decision to make. They could stick with their routine of panning for gold in the summer, or expand to a larger sluicing operation with equipment, hoping to extract more than just nuggets. Both her brother-in-law and his son had other business interests, so they had just carried on the panning along the creek, enjoying it as a summer activity. Expanding the operation might produce a real profit, but it would also require more investment and probably hiring some other people to help, as well as alerting possible competitors who lived locally and who might try to help themselves during the weeks outside of the summer season.

The Countess had left it up to them, and agreed that they should continue on as in past years to see what the future would bring. She was now happily receiving a significant return from the gold to meet her need for revenge. Looking at the glittering nuggets had been satisfying. She would fly to Whitehorse every two years and pick up the nuggets, wrap them as candies in chocolate boxes, and pack them in her suitcase. Who would bother an elderly woman bringing back chocolates? And Whitehorse, being part of Canada, had no U.S. Customs to clear. She had a safety deposit box in Vancouver, but never declared the value of the nuggets, of course, as panning for gold was a "hobby" in her mind, and not subject to tax. Somewhat akin to Midas, she enjoyed visiting the bank, opening the box, and counting her treasure.

The Countess put the suitcase next to her other one in the closet, keeping the key in her cosmetic bag just in case Annie became curious. Perhaps she would just take this trip again as a way to collect the gold. Though she would pass through U.S. Customs when the ship arrived back in Vancouver, the Countess had heard that a search, if any, was very cursory, because everyone was trying to disembark so that new passengers could board. Looking out the window, she saw blue sky, so she decided to take a walk and ponder the new value of her gowns.

Chapter 18

Olive looked across at Karen as the women set into their sandwiches back aboard the ship; they had more than an hour to kill before taking the streetcar tour. Without Jack to stifle any opinions she might venture, Karen was a completely different person—engaging and interesting, with an unexpected wit. She seemed now to want to apologize for Jack, telling the women some interesting stories about their college days, where, clearly, she had been infatuated with his big-man-on-campus status, and had married him before she really got to know him better.

Reading between the lines, so to speak, and hearing her sigh, it was obvious that the reality of married life had left her less than misty-eyed; Olive had seen her chafe plenty under his scrutiny and criticism.

Karen also became a different person when speaking about her son, and although Jack Jr. had followed his father into the insurance business, it was easy to see from her description of him that he was more his mother's son. *Well, good for him*, Olive thought. Hopefully he and his girlfriend, whom Karen liked, would marry and give her a grandchild to dote on.

"So, what should I buy Chantelle for a souvenir?" Maggie's question brought Olive back from her reverie. Maggie's daughter was hard to buy for, but probably would appreciate something truly representative of the trip.

"What about a Native print, and then you can get it framed back in Queens?" Jean offered in response.

"And maybe one of those wool hats from Vancouver, like the sweater Olive is buying Howard?"

Karen glanced at her watch. "Probably time to get going."

Back on shore Olive started laughing. "Well, no one will run into us on this streetcar," she said, pointing at a bright yellow vehicle pulling up to the stop. A woman dressed in a period costume from around the turn of the century walked down the steps, smiling at the group assembled nearby.

"Come along, everyone," she called. "I'm Melinda, and for the next hour or so, we are going back in history to early Skagway to talk about the cast of characters which made it what it is today."

As people settled themselves into their seats and the streetcar eased out toward the city street, Melinda began her narrative. "To begin with, you're riding in a vehicle of presidential significance," she announced from the front of the streetcar. "President Hardy himself was the first to ride the streetcar during his visit here in 1923. As you can see, a lot of the downtown buildings also date back many years. These six blocks constitute the Skagway Historic District. As part of the plan to bring tourists in, the buildings have been preserved or restored to showcase the downtown in its glory around the turn of the last century. There are shops of all kinds, and many of the buildings have wonderful black-and-white photos of the town and its people at the time. We won't stop here because we have a big area to cover, but you can always just stroll back yourselves. I believe your ship doesn't depart until nine o'clock."

Olive mused as they rolled past the harbor toward the overlook just off the Klondike Highway. To see a community so dependent on the gold rush and on tourism, relying on foodstuffs arriving by boat and dealing with the long, cold winters, would take someone with either a very good job or a truly adventurous spirit to call this home. As though reading her thoughts, Melinda answered all of her unspoken questions, telling them that yes, the cost of living was quite high and the winters were long, but the community itself was vibrant and she wouldn't think of living anywhere else.

The tour took them by the modest home where Governor Palin apparently spent part of her childhood. As with the guide in Juneau, Melinda chuckled and told the passengers that, in fact, "you cannot see Russia from here." Then it was on to the Gold Rush Cemetery, where "Soapy" Smith and some other characters were buried. The tour ended with the view from the overlook, which was absolutely stunning. It occurred to Olive that so far, the weather had held—such a blessing!

Chapter 19

Jack smirked as he and Bev drove their cart up to the clubhouse. "Well, this isn't much of a golf course, but I still got it, don't you think?" he said. As no one was watching, he reached over and gave Bev a kiss. "I wonder if old Art is enjoying his hike?"

Bev squeezed Jack's hand. "That sandwich you picked up from the kitchen was good, but a quiet, cold beer right now would also hit the spot. We don't have to rush back to the ship anyhow, and I'm enjoying the time alone with you."

Jack's chest puffed out almost beyond his belly. "Sure thing, babe. I imagine Karen is regaling those other broads with all kinds of stories I can do without." Jack tapped the ash off his cigar onto the pavement by the clubhouse while Bev took out a cigarette. "Tomorrow will be a drag, because we spend most of it going around in circles in a bay somewhere, watching parts of glaciers fall into the water. Yawn. But tonight should be alright; we can hit the casino right after dinner. No doubt Karen and Art will go for that quiz in the pub."

Bev giggled. "Maybe while they're listening to questions in the pub, you can come to our suite and we can find some answers of our own?"

Jack fondled her knee. "Would love to, but we'd better cool it until we get back to New York. The last thing we need is for either Art or Karen to come looking for us."

Jack's gaze lingered for a moment. He thought about meeting Bev for the first time, watching her more than listening to her presentation about 401K retirement plans. He had been captivated from the start, because while she was professional, she was very attentive to him, touching him on the arm a couple of times and laughing at his jokes. Bev was trim and athletic, almost as tall as he was, and liked golf.

While he had wooed Karen when they were both young and in college, and had enjoyed her being petite, and, of course, in need of his protection, he found their marriage had grown stale over the years. She was always after him to try new things, go to concerts and museums, that kind of stuff. If the woman had only learned to golf, he probably wouldn't have fallen for Bev. Or at least that's what he told himself.

"Penny for your thoughts, or maybe a beer?" Bev tapped him lightly on the shoulder.

She still found herself trying to figure Jack out. She liked that he was so dynamic, but sometimes he lapsed into long silences. Art wasn't that talkative, either, but he always tried to get her interested in the news and history—his subject while teaching—while she just wanted him to shut up and finish his dinner so she could watch sports or a reality show on the tube. Thank God they had two televisions so he could watch something he liked and leave her alone. She loved their son, Matt, but if not for him, she would never have married Art.

"Well, we'd better get back to the ship." Jack snorted while taking a last gulp of beer from the bottle. "If we're lucky, Karen and her gang will have already started on their tour around Skagway, so we won't be pestered to go along. I wouldn't mind some time by the pool."

They arrived at the dock to some commotion next to the gangplank. Jack spotted Karen talking to a fellow in uniform, so they walked over. "What's up? I thought the ship didn't leave until late tonight?" he said.

"Oh, Jack!" Karen exclaimed. "Art told us he'd be back by now, but we can't find him. Bev, we just came from your suite, but he isn't answering, so we think he's not there." The women beside her nodded their heads in unison.

"I'll go on board and check," Bev responded. "Jack, do you want to come with me?"

"No, I'll stay with the girls. Or better yet, why don't we go into the pool lounge and wait there? I could do with a gin and tonic."

The group dispersed while Olive exchanged glances with Jean. She whispered, "They don't look worried about it, but Art's been out for a long time."

Bev let herself into her suite and looked in the closet to see if Art's hiking boots were there. They weren't. There was no evidence of a recent shower, either, so she took the elevator and walked through the library area in case he had stopped there. No sign of him there, either, so she walked to the pool area and spotted Jack with the other women, ordering beverages.

"It looks like he hasn't come back to the suite yet," she said, accepting a gin and tonic from Jack.

Jack glanced over at Olive, who was pulling the hat she bought Howard out of her bag. "Let's see that," he said, and tried it on, moving it to one side to look jaunty. "Karen, you should have bought one for me to wear on the golf course!"

Karen shrugged, not telling her husband that she had bought one for Jack Jr., along with the video to show both of them. Let them figure it out when she got home.

Half an hour passed and there was still no sign of Art. Suddenly, they saw two uniformed officers approach them, with a crew member pointing in their direction.

The crew member spoke first. "Mrs. Herrington?" he addressed Bev. "Did your husband Arthur go on a hike today? We don't have him listed on any of the excursions, but he appears to have departed the ship at the same time you did this morning."

"Why yes!" Bev answered. "I went golfing. He often likes to hike back home and didn't want to join the other tours. Is he alright? He does have a heart problem, but he takes medication every morning."

The officer spoke next. "Ma'am, I'm sorry to tell you this, but a group of hikers came upon his body about a mile out of town. Looks like your husband was probably coming down from Sturgil's Landing. The hikers had actually walked up to the Landing with him and said he was fine. But when they found him, according to one of the hikers, he had apparently collapsed beside the trail, like he'd suffocated or had a heart attack. An ambulance has taken him to the morgue so one of the local doctors can examine him and sign the death certificate. Usually the doctor will then call the coroner's office for further instructions. If you come with me, I need you to identify him. I'm so sorry for your loss."

Bev sat there, looking stunned. Karen put her arm around her and everyone, even Jack, was quiet.

Then Jack asked, "Bev, do you want me to come along for moral support? I can call Matt, if you want. I'm sure he'll tell you to stay on the ship, rather than fly home alone. We can also find out what the morgue wants to do with Art."

Olive gazed at Jack. He was certainly a take-charge kind of fellow, and didn't seem fazed at all that Art had died. Bev hadn't shed a tear, but maybe it was the shock. Olive watched her lean into Jack's chest while

Karen's eyes appeared to narrow as she looked at the two of them.

Olive then asked the officer, "Was the hike Art took particularly strenuous?"

"Not particularly, ma'am," he answered. "It's a good four to five hours, but popular with the locals. If Mr. Herrington was an experienced hiker, he should have been alright."

Olive caught Jack looking over at her, his jaw appearing to clench.

Jack motioned to the officer. "If you can wait here for a few minutes, I'm going to go to our suite to pick up my phone so I can call Bev's son. I forgot it this morning."

Jack entered his suite and sat by the writing desk. He couldn't help but smile. "So Bev is a widow now? How about that!"

Chapter 20

The Countess left her suite and took the elevator to the promenade deck. Walking out into the mild breeze reminded her of her honeymoon voyage—the surprisingly calm Atlantic crossing, enjoying sunny walks on her husband's arm. Now she couldn't help but scoff at the attire of others on the promenade.

So sloppy! she huffed to herself. In my day people dressed up to travel, particularly on luxury liners—no shorts and sandals.

But enough of that. She returned to happier thoughts, remembering the train ride to Paris after disembarking from the ocean liner on the coast of France, seeing the sights in Paris, and learning from the Count's narrative. While he was very patient in squiring her around the city, it was clear that he was anxious to return to his ancestral home in Germany, to visit his widowed mother and younger brother. Viewing the countryside from the train had been wonderful, especially as it neared Bavaria, and she felt very grand indeed when her husband lifted her into a carriage at the station.

The carriage took them into the Bavarian countryside, which, surprisingly, appeared to have been spared Allied bombing from just a couple of years before. Farmers were working in their fields, gathering hay for the coming winter, and the Countess could see milk cows lumbering back toward their barns. Her husband sat quietly in contemplation of the post-war conditions, and then, breaking his silence, told her that he and his younger brother had been sent out of the country to work with their father in Alaska, and so had escaped conscription into Hitler's army.

Her husband said that he marveled at his mother's stubbornness; she'd refused to leave the old property, keeping it afloat with the help of a couple of older retainers. But by war's end, when his father elected to return, leaving his sons in Alaska to carry on the logging business, the estate, while not crumbling, was in need of many repairs. Unfortunately, he died suddenly after only one year at home. The Count stayed in Alaska, while his younger brother took the long journey back home to console their mother. The Count's young bride would meet both of them that day.

Even with her husband's description, arriving at the Count's castle was something of a disappointment, she remembered; she had been expecting a more palatial setting. The estate had obviously boasted beautiful gardens at one time, which would have taken a lot of manpower—manpower now lost in the war—and although the home was, indeed, a castle of sorts, it could not rival the photographs of castles along the Rhine.

It was clear that, while her new husband possessed an old title and an estate, cold hard cash must have been wanting, as everything appeared still in need of an upgrade. The Countess loved her husband and was grateful for her new title, but she was even more grateful for the funds she would receive from her father. The Countess was too used to the security of her family to do without it in her marriage.

She continued her walk along the deck, turning at the bow to view the shore from the starboard side. On this side of the ship she felt more exposed, the freshening breeze causing her to quicken her pace. Realizing that her experience in the interior of the ship had been limited to the dining room and the library area, she decided to escape the chilly breeze and enjoy another cup of tea at one of the tables in the public area.

Seating herself and motioning to a crew member, she thought she saw a familiar figure. Indeed, it was her maid, Annie, walking along to greet an Asian man who appeared to have just returned to the ship, as he was putting an identification badge in his pocket.

The fact that Annie touched his arm in response to his grin gave the Countess pause. Who was this man, and how would Annie know him? She had kept Annie rather isolated from the time of her "adoption," not wanting her to get ideas about a possible life outside of the Countess' employment. Had Annie looked her way, she would have motioned to her, telling her to join her at the table, but Annie and the fellow had already turned away, appearing to head outdoors. She would question Annie closely when she returned to the suite.

At that moment, An could not have been happier. Li-Liang was attentive to her as he guided her to the promenade deck, and since she had not seen her employer sitting in the public area, An had not a care in the world.

She asked Li-Liang if he had been able to leave the ship.

"Yes, for a little while," he replied. "I did not want to ride the bus tour around the town, so I took a stroll there instead."

An laughed. "Well, what a surprise! I did the same thing, but did not see you there."

Li-Liang looked startled. "We must have just missed each other. Let's finish our walk and then go to the pool area for a beer. I will pay."

An giggled. "That will be the second beer on this trip! I'd better be careful."

At a table near the pool, the couple fell into conversation. This time, Li-Liang not only asked questions about the Countess, but about An herself. She told him how lonely she often felt, always at her employer's beck and call. He asked her why she had not gone on the train trip with her mistress.

"She wanted me to stay here and wait to meet her when the trip was over. I am just a beast of burden to her," An said sourly. "But a man met her when the train arrived—apparently some relative of hers—and gave her a suitcase. The Countess had me carry it. It was a little heavy, but to have me wait around just to carry the suitcase wasn't very fair."

Li-Liang raised his eyebrows and leaned forward. "That is strange. Why would a relative meet the Countess, just to give her a suitcase?"

An nodded. "Yes, it *was* strange, especially because he isn't from around here. I heard him say that he had to return to the Yukon on a motor coach. Maybe he brought her a bunch of gold!" She giggled.

In response, Li-Liang asked another question very quietly: "Does the Countess remain in her cabin all the time?"

An gave him a brief summary of her schedule.

"Have you seen where she put the suitcase?" Li-Liang asked.

At that moment, there was some commotion near the pool. Two police officers had entered with a crew member and were walking toward a group of people having cocktails. Whatever the police told them brought an immediate reaction from group, obviously one of shock and grief.

They heard one of the officers say that a group of hikers had found him, whoever "he" was, but at that point, Li-Liang began to rise, telling An that he had to use the bathroom in his cabin, and would probably see her sometime later. An was left to finish her beer alone before returning to her employer's suite.

Chapter 21

Karen stayed with the women while Jack and Bev accompanied the officers to the morgue. "I just can't believe that Art is dead!" she gasped. "He always takes good care of himself, watches his weight and all of that. It doesn't seem fair."

Olive nodded. "Such a nice man, too. It will be an adjustment for Bev. I remember feeling so lost when Bill died suddenly of a heart attack. I was so thankful to have my son and his wife, good friends in the community, and my faith to see me through. And after a year, I moved to New York and had Jean and Maggie, and, of course, now Howard—I was so blessed."

Jean reached over and took Olive's hand, watching her tear up just a little.

Karen sat quietly for a moment. "I'm sorry to think this way, but I wonder how much Bev will actually miss Art. We've been at their home for drinks a couple of times and they seem to lead parallel lives, but then, who am I to talk? Jack's life revolves around his business and golf, and he has our son *in* the business, so Jack Jr. probably sees more of him than I do . . ." She trailed off, then muttered, "And frankly, with Art gone, I wouldn't be surprised if Bev and Jack golf together even more, so . . ."

Maggie spoke up. "But it looks like you do some interesting things on your own?"

"Oh, yes," Karen responded. "I have friends, and Jack Jr. doesn't like golf, so he and I enjoy outings to Manhattan. And to be fair to Jack, he likes to dance, so we'll go to the country club dances, and sometimes take the train into the city for Broadway shows. It isn't like we do nothing together." She paused. "Anyway, I think I'll go to our suite for a rest before dinner. If you don't see us, don't worry. We may just ask Bev to join us for some room service."

The women watched Karen move through the Lido deck toward the elevators.

Olive ventured, "I could probably use a nap, too, but I'm going to stop by the library first, so feel free to go on without me."

Jean looked at Maggie. "I don't like the look of this. Just what are you planning to research, Olive?" she demanded.

Olive looked sheepish. "I'm not sure. How could Art just die like that? They didn't say that he choked on anything. So I'm just curious, okay?"

The day before, Olive had been browsing through the library, looking for a British mystery, some good skulduggery without too much blood, and had been surprised at what the library had to offer—not only fiction, but non-fiction and reference texts, and even an old set of the Encyclopedia Britannia.

Now she looked up the index categories and found "poisons," and then retrieved the appropriate volume. She considered taking it to the suite, but thought better of it, as she could already hear the teasing from Jean and Maggie.

No wonder Agatha Christie favored poisons for many of her murders! There were certainly a lot of them, both synthetic and natural. Hemlock, of course, as well as belladonna. There was a description of tetrodotoxin, from the pufferfish. Cyanide was found in household products and killed quickly. Olive remembered reading about Jim Jones' colony years ago, where he had his followers drink Kool-Aid laced with the stuff. What a horrible way to go!

She looked through the description of arsenic, which, according to the article, at one time was foolproof and undetectable, until some fellow in the mid-1800s named Marsh came up with a test for it used in post-mortems. Apparently, you could even kill someone with botulinum toxin, which causes the paralysis of the respiratory system—a rather slow way to die. The article mentioned that this substance was used in Botox, which made Olive chuckle—oh, well, at least you wouldn't have any wrinkles when you croaked!

But the item that caught her attention was particularly chilling. A poison derived from the plant sometimes called monkshood, sometimes wolfsbane, was particularly dangerous. In nature, touching the leaves without gloves could be fatal. The poison itself was called aconite and was used by some early warriors to poison arrow tips for battle and for killing predator animals like wolves. *And* it could be added to food.

She read on. Apparently, the Roman emperor Claudius had been felled by mushrooms prepared by his wife, Agrippa, who had lovingly included wolfsbane in her recipe. Yikes! Victims of aconite poisoning suffered asphyxia from arrhythmic heart function, and the poison didn't show up in an autopsy, although apparently, if injected, it could show up in a blood test.

Olive looked up from her reading. No, this couldn't be. Not in this day and age. But the hikers said that Art looked like he had suffocated or had a heart attack, and she had witnessed Jack stuffing a sandwich into Art's backpack as they left the ship. She supposed that if the sandwich was slathered with very spicy mustard or some other condiment, Art would be none the wiser.

The last item in the article mentioned that aconite was, in fact, available in the U.S., often through Asian herbalists, as it was thought to be therapeutic in small doses. Would Jack go to such lengths?

Olive shook herself. Oh, come on, girl; you're letting your imagination run wild! She had no evidence that Bev and Jack were romantically involved, and even if they were, divorce today was much simpler than murder, for heaven's sake!

She closed the encyclopedia firmly and put it back on the shelf. Ever since that Kinfolk business she had found herself more suspicious, more observant of people's behaviors—and she found this change unsettling. Olive resolved to keep her thoughts to herself, knowing that Jean and Maggie would think she had lost her mind.

As she turned to leave, she caught sight of the Camera Man standing by the entrance, looking in her direction. He then turned suddenly, and walked swiftly down the hall. Olive shook herself slightly, murmuring that she should stop reading mysteries.

Chapter 22

When Olive opened the door to the suite, she found both Maggie and Jean snoring quietly. Not wanting to disturb them, she let herself out onto the veranda. The shoreline was busy with people coming back from tours, and the souvenir shops were doing a brisk business.

It seemed like days ago, rather than just this morning, that Karen had joined them in the train trip and the streetcar ride. Olive felt sad about Art, but she did want to continue to enjoy this once-in-a-lifetime trip, and she felt sure that Jean and Maggie agreed. It was also clear that, while Karen was an empathetic person who had liked Art and would try to console Bev, she and Bev had little in common except for Jack. Olive resolved to continue her new friendship with Karen, and to give her the opportunity to continue with the pub quiz and other activities, if she wished.

Hearing a snuffling behind her, she turned back to the room to watch Jean stretch out like a cat and slink out of bed. Stifling a yawn herself, Olive started to move back into the room. Seeing that Maggie was still sleeping, Jean just motioned for Olive to stay seated and joined her on the veranda.

"You should probably have a nap too," Jean whispered. When Olive shook her head, Jean continued, "So what do you make of all this?"

Olive whispered in response, "You'll think I'm nuts, but the library research produced some interesting stuff." Seeing Jean roll her eyes, Olive continued, "No, wait! I'm serious."

Knowing that Olive's suspicions of Mr. Barnes in the Kinfolk matter had been correct, Jean held her tongue, motioning for her twin sister to continue.

Olive recounted what she had learned about aconite, and how it was possible that Art had eaten it in the sandwich. It all seemed too coincidental to be an accident.

Jean nodded. "That's pretty brazen, assuming that Jack and/or Bev are the culprits. But if the poison won't show on an autopsy, what do you really have?" she asked. "And if it *is* true, then I'd be worried about Karen for the rest of the cruise. Jack may decide to go for broke—I somehow can't place Bev as part of the poisoning—but I could imagine Jack trying his luck again."

Olive sighed. "I hadn't thought of that. We can't make any accusations without proof, and Karen doesn't have a heart problem, so faking heart arrhythmia as the cause isn't in play for her. But remember the first night at dinner? Jack mentioned her EpiPen. Let's talk to Karen alone and find out the severity of her allergies, that sort of thing."

They heard stirring in the room, then Maggie's bark out to the veranda: "What are you two plotting out there?"

Laughing, they both moved inside while Maggie called room service for some ice. Over cocktails, Jean wondered aloud whether they should eat in the dining room or try room service for dinner.

"I'd like to try all of the dining room dinners, but room service might be interesting, too," Olive said. "And I guess it's tomorrow night that the captain hosts the dinner—the food is supposed to be awesome, so we have to go to that. I'll check tonight's menu posted outside the dining room so we can decide for tonight."

With that, Olive slipped out the door and walked to the elevator. As the elevator doors opened, Jack and Bev strode out, just about knocking Olive over. No apologies were forthcoming.

Olive caught Bev's eye and asked how she was doing.

Bev muttered, "There's so much paperwork and so many questions. They won't release Art's body for the time being, so I can't get him cremated, because the coroner is considering an autopsy. That one hiker has got them thinking that because Art was 'fine' when he was in their company, that his 'sudden death may have to be investigated.' Jack called Matt, and Matt said I should stay on the ship and he'll fly to meet me in Vancouver, but I think Jack convinced him to stay put and I'll fly back with Karen and Jack. Jack told Matt I'll need him all the more when we get back to New York. I'm actually going to give Matt a call when I get to our suite."

Jack joined in. "Karen and I are going to have Bev eat room service with us. Are you and the other ladies planning on doing the pub quiz tonight? I can see if Karen wants to join you while I take Bev to the casino to get her mind off of things."

Olive ventured that they probably would go to the pub and they would all be welcome to join them, but Jack and Bev exchanged glances. Bev replied that she really didn't feel up to fun stuff like that right now.

Olive breathed a quiet sigh of relief. She couldn't imagine anything *less* fun than a team involving Jack and Bev, and this way they could get some more information from Karen about her allergies.

Later, looking at the menu on the wall next to the restaurant, Olive was torn about whether to dine there that night, but the night's food did skew towards Asian cuisine, and she didn't really feel in the mood for it. She'd report back to Maggie and Jean, but wouldn't be surprised if room service was their choice. It had been a hectic day.

While Olive napped, Maggie and Jean took turns taking showers.

The ship's television had local features and information about Glacier Bay, tomorrow's destination. The room service menu appeared adequate, but for obvious reasons, it was not as gourmet as the offerings in the dining room. But Jean and Maggie were able to have steak sandwiches and cold beer, while Olive opted for chicken marsala with red wine.

At fifteen minutes to eight, they knocked on the door to the Leonards' suite to see if Karen wished to join them in the pub. Opening the door, Karen invited them in and they gazed around the room. The suite was much like theirs, although a little smaller, and they had obviously also just completed a room service dinner. Jack was cradling a scotch while Bev was lying back on the couch, sipping some white wine.

Karen responded tentatively, "I guess I might as well join you. Jack and Bev plan to win some money at the casino tonight and I don't want to stay here alone, so thanks for the invitation."

There was an awkward silence as Jack just stared out the window while Bev focused on her wine glass. Maggie looked at her watch and suggested they get going.

The pub was as noisy as usual, and two Australians waved at them frantically to join them. When they sat down, Olive asked them about Arnie and Alice, as she hadn't seen them around at all.

One of the Aussies replied, "We popped by on the way down here and they're both sick as dingos! Both of them, alternating on the toilet and being sick in a bucket! And Alice is a nurse, for Gawd's sake! I told them if they don't call the ship's doctor, we will—this is no way to spend an anniversary."

The other Aussie, slurring a little, yelled, "Where's Art?"

Olive put her hand on his arm to quiet him somewhat. "Art died today on a hike outside of town."

The Aussie paled, suddenly sober. "Oh my Gawd! We heard someone had an accident, but that was it. Was he married?"

The women looked at each other, not sure whether it was their place to give too much backstory. Just then, the quizmaster boomed, "Are you ready to answer some questions?"

The time passed quickly and as they had come to expect, the quiz was a lot of fun. Karen appeared to relax and contribute answers, but it did seem strange to all of them that Art wasn't there to add his knowledge of history and science.

Afterward, Karen eagerly accepted the trio's invitation to join them in the jazz lounge, while the Australians, not unexpectedly, opted to stay with "some mates" in the pub. Olive was glad, as the quiet atmosphere would allow for some conversation, and maybe some insight into Karen's medical condition.

As they sat down, the ship quietly pulled away from the dock and they took the time to look out the windows at the lights of Skagway. Olive shuddered to think about Art, laid out on a table in the morgue, and wondered whether the local authorities would choose an autopsy or decide to just close the matter as a natural death. It occurred to her that Karen might know, so she asked.

"Jack and Bev weren't sure, and they didn't want to miss the ship's departure," Karen informed her. "The police officer assured them that it was just standard procedure to leave the body for the time being, as there was no coroner immediately available. Bev identified Art and was told the ship would be contacted as to whether she should get off in Ketchikan to answer any further questions. She and Jack were golfing at the time, so I don't know what she can add, but I suppose the police want to 'cover all their bases,' so to speak.

"You know, I feel so badly for Art. He so looked forward to that hike, and it appears to be what killed him. He also mentioned Glacier Bay a couple of times, where everyone on board would get a chance to see icebergs calving into the water. And him being an environmentalist of sorts—to see the shrinking of the glaciers firsthand, not just on television documentaries. It's depressing to know that there won't be much ice left in a couple of generations. I just hope that Jack keeps his mouth shut. It gets even more depressing to hear how ignorant he can sound, especially when I know he's intelligent enough to understand climate change and all that. Sometimes I think he enjoys the attention he gets by being a flat-earth kind of guy."

Maggie jumped in. "You're certainly welcome to join us for Glacier Bay, either in our suite or on the upper deck. We'll probably do a little of both. Why don't we trade cell phone numbers so we can keep in touch tomorrow?"

Their cocktails arrived and they all sat back to listen to the soothing jazz quintet. At the break, Olive asked Karen if she had enjoyed the room service, and found out that she, Jack, and Bev concurred with Olive that room service was alright, but the dining room—particularly tomorrow night's dinner with the captain—was far superior.

"Jack mentioned once that you have allergies," Olive followed up. "Are they related to food?"

Karen sighed. "They have been the bane of my existence, from early childhood on. Nuts can kill me, that's how severe my condition is. My poor parents, so vigilant to protect me, and I, of course, as an adult, having to be so watchful—thank heaven for EpiPens! I always carry one with me and pack two or three in my suitcase, but, knock on wood, I haven't had any incident in a while. It's easier to control when I cook at home, but restaurants can be tricky. Jack gets so impatient when I double-check ingredients, but he doesn't understand the terror I feel when my throat starts to constrict."

Jean ventured, "I suppose one thing about nuts is that they're pretty easy to taste, as opposed to soybeans or eggs, that sort of thing?"

Karen shook her head. "You'd be surprised. It takes so little to set me off, and I do like spicy food, which can mask the flavor. That's why I grill the waiter sometimes if we're in an Asian restaurant, for instance. Jack Jr. loves Asian cuisine, so when he and I visit Manhattan, he always wants to go to certain restaurants. But if I have my EpiPen handy, I'm not as concerned."

Maggie looked around the table. They had all finished their cocktails, so she stood up, telling them that she was heading to the room. "Since we don't leave the ship tomorrow I'm going to get out one of the DVDs and watch some guilty pleasure before turning in," she announced.

The other women murmured in agreement, so Karen stood as well, looking a little wistful. "Maybe I'll walk over to the casino to see if Jack and Bev are still there," she sighed.

Chapter 23

That evening, the Countess looked around the dining room, hearing the soft music, the rustle of linens, and the gentle clink of silverware and serving dishes. *One thing she did not hear,* she thought with a sigh, was the booming voice of that American man who always sat with his wife and another couple—and sometimes with that nice woman, Olive, and her sister and friend. While the Countess would have enjoyed a true dinner companion—not a servant like Annie, but a friend and peer—she shuddered at the notion of being that close to the American man's voice and bad manners.

Perhaps the group had decided on room service, she thought, although she couldn't understand why. The menu tonight had a more Asian theme, it was true, but the choices looked delicious. No doubt Annie would like it, although the Countess didn't bother to ask her.

When Annie had returned to the suite this afternoon, she had managed to wake the Countess from a nap. When she tried to back out of the room, her employer, now fully awake but cranky, had called her over. "I see that you have found a friend on this cruise, or is it someone you knew beforehand?" the Countess asked.

Annie had looked both guilty and afraid, raising the Countess' suspicions even further. "I just met him recently, when I was walking on the deck," Annie had replied. "He is also from China. He is a nice man."

The Countess had taken An's response to mean that Li-Liang was a Chinese tourist, and An was not going to disabuse her of that notion. True, Li-Liang had been questioning her about the Countess' financial situation, particularly after she told him about the suitcase that afternoon, but An just put that down as natural curiosity.

Now, while the Countess sipped her wine, An noticed Li-Liang entering the dining room. Again, he took a small table that gave him a clear view of their sitting area.

Her employer, always alert, also saw the man enter and take a seat. She smirked at An. "Well, it looks like your boyfriend is hungry, too!" she cackled.

An grimaced. "He is not my boyfriend." She thought sourly that the Countess, having no real joy in her life, made sure that An's life was equally joyless. Had she been the Countess, she would have invited Li-Liang to join them, knowing he would otherwise eat alone. But then, she thought it better that her employer believed him to be a Chinese tourist. That would make it much easier for the couple to meet without too much suspicion from the Countess. Dinner conversation would only reveal that he, too, lived in Vancouver.

Li-Liang reviewed the menu after he ordered a beer. Ah, Asian food on the menu tonight! He didn't mind Western food, but watching a lot of overweight men sawing on huge chunks of steak or prime rib almost made him nauseous. He chuckled to himself, thinking about how many in a village in Asia could feast on such large portions of beef.

Again, Li-Liang couldn't help but be shocked by the relationship, or lack of one, between An Lee and the Countess. In the short time he had gotten to know An, he had been struck by how eager she was to please, a characteristic which her employer obviously took for granted. The girl was also very open—*too open, probably,* he thought, remembering all she had told him about the Countess during their short visits.

So, the old woman might be carrying some valuables? Hmm. That she would be picking up a suitcase from someone possibly related to her in Skagway, of all places, and if, as An had reported, the fellow was "returning to the Yukon," it could mean that the contents of the suitcase might have some significance. But, on the other hand, perhaps it just contained family mementos or the like. Li-Liang's mind raced at the possibilities.

Coming into a lot of money would cement his future, but how should he go about it? He could try to persuade An to let him into their suite—she must have her own key—but he would have to be very careful, as he guessed that An was deathly afraid of angering the Countess. If An was now a Canadian citizen, Li-Liang thought, she wouldn't have to fear deportment if her employer leveled any theft charges against her, but she could also go to jail, or at least face unemployment and homelessness.

He shrugged to himself, knowing that there were still several days left on the voyage, enough time to see how much of a risk An would take. Looking up, he saw both An and the Countess staring at him, so he gave them his most engaging smile.

Chapter 24

Alice had never been this sick in her life. Watching Arnie as they alternated between the toilet and the ice bucket they were using to vomit into made her want to sob. They were both experiencing abdominal pain, although she suspected that it was related to the diarrhea, and their headaches were getting worse, hardly responding to the aspirin at all.

Maybe it was as simple as the flu, because they did have fevers, both of them—she knew that without using a thermometer. Alice was beginning to feel like she was dreaming while she was still half-awake, memories flooding in about first meeting Arnie, and their time together in Africa. While they were both from Australia, they hadn't met until their work in Gabon had brought them together. They'd laughed at the irony of that, both growing up in the Sydney area without ever crossing paths. Arnie had trained to be an engineer and she had graduated from nursing school. It was his mates' request that they join them on the cruise, and Alice had been happy to meet them. She felt sorry for Arnie, as whatever had afflicted them both was preventing him from spending much time with them. Hopefully this too would pass.

Her mind drifted back to Gabon itself, where they were introduced to each other in the capital of Libreville. Together, they would go out as a team to help with local medical treatment and to build wells and more sanitary systems in the smaller villages. The three days in the capital allowed them to adjust to the time change, and the team went out for dinner on two of the evenings to get to know one another—particularly since Adam, the third member of the team, was from Holland.

They all shared their idealism, knowing that they could have chosen to stay in their respective countries, with all the comforts of the first world and bright futures in their professions. But they all shared a desire to "make a difference," even a small one, by doing service in remote areas of the world—at least for a while. They also knew that they must acclimatize quickly to the culture of the village, while trying to introduce modern customs related to health and prevention of disease.

Arriving by jeep in the village, they had been struck by the beauty of the scenery and the absolute verdant foliage—even spotting a huge waterfall in the distance. The leaders in the villages provided them with primitive accommodations: a hut for the men to share and a separate hut for Alice.

The first night had been a culture shock, watching the men in the village slaughter a goat in their honor, being shown the latrine near the village and the huts where they would sleep for most of the next year. For the most part, they would only leave the village to go out into even more remote areas, bringing medical supplies and testing the water. They were also allowed to come back to Libreville every two months to pick up supplies and get a day or two of R and R by the beach. Thank goodness Libreville was a coastal city! Having come from Sydney, both Arnie and Alice looked forward to jumping in the Atlantic a few times. Adam looked forward to that, too.

While Alice had been a dedicated and apt nursing student, nothing could have prepared her for nursing the villagers through their myriad illnesses and infections, some just arising from a failure to visit her clinic. She had antibiotics available and other medical supplies at the ready, and hoped to teach the people, especially the women, that vaccinations and other preventative measures could save their children from disease.

The village was the first place where she actually witnessed a death, something she'd wondered how she'd been able to avoid during her training. But she also experienced her first birth, too, just before she and Arnie had left on this trip to Alaska. As harrowing as the experience had been—more so for the mother, of course—Alice felt like she was really serving that community.

As the months in the village had gone by, she'd adjusted to the pressure of the work, allowing her to spend more time with Arnie and Adam. Although Alice liked Adam and respected his commitment to the project, she'd found herself drawn to Arnie from the beginning. Not only was he handsome, but he had a presence about him, a quiet authority she felt would be appreciated by the people they were trying to help. He also had a great sense of humor—a must in any man she might consider. *It could get you through a lot of situations,* she mused. Unfortunately this situation was not one of them.

Arnie came out of the bathroom and climbed back into bed. "Well, babe, what should we do?" he asked. "This is going on too long to be a case of flu. Let's call the doctor and tell him our symptoms over the phone so he can decide whether to make a house call, shall we?"

"You're right!" Alice responded. "We can't go on without some help or the trip will be over before we know it."

The ship's doctor took the call from Alice and made notes while she gave him their symptoms. After she had finished, he responded, "Whatever you have, it sounds serious. Hopefully, it isn't contagious. I'll come to your cabin. Just open your door and get back into bed. I should be there shortly."

Taking a surgical mask, a pair of latex gloves, and his medical kit with him, the doctor entered the cabin. He closed the door behind him and took the chair near the desk. "I'm Dr. Benson and I want you just to lie there while I get some further information," he introduced himself. "I'll pass over the thermometer. Alice, take your temperature and give it back to me so I can sterilize it before passing it on to your husband. Although you've probably cross contaminated yourselves anyway by now," he chuckled.

Alice took her temperature, followed by Arnie, with the doctor writing down their temperatures after each test.

His face showed concern when he read out the temperatures. "Who started to feel unwell first—or was it simultaneous?" he asked.

He nodded when Alice ventured that she probably began feeling unwell a day or so before Arnie, although at first she thought it was just jet lag from the long trip from Africa.

Dr. Benson visibly started at that information. "Whereabouts in Africa?"

"Gabon, on the west coast," Arnie responded. "The country is just west of the Congo and we've been there about eighteen months. We were part of a team working in a remote area. About a year ago we got married, and we're on this cruise to celebrate our first anniversary with a couple of my mates from Australia." Anticipating the doctor's next question, Arnie continued. "We've hardly seen anything of them, though, as we haven't felt like socializing. We've been pretty much just lying here in bed, eating a little room service and drinking water, hoping to keep some of it down."

"Did you have vaccinations before you left for Africa?" Dr. Benson asked.

"I know we both had malaria shots and I assume we were both good on other stuff," Arnie answered. "We never felt sick while we were in the village—it was only after we left on our trip to Canada that we started to feel bad. I'll look in our luggage to check whether we brought our medical records with us."

The doctor got both Arnie and Alice to recount their duties, and asked Alice in particular if she always used gloves when working with patients.

She thought back. "I'm pretty sure I did, but I remember helping with a childbirth just before my departure, and it all happened so fast that I didn't get a chance to glove up."

"Were there any indications of your symptoms among the villagers before you left?" Dr. Benson asked. I'm not trying to alarm you, but you appear to be worse off than simple flu, and you *have* come from the part of Africa where the Ebola virus has struck in the past."

Both Alice and Arnie bent forward on the bed, stunned.

Arnie spoke first. "I can't believe that. We've been out of the village just a week or so. You'd think the locals would have shown signs that would have alerted us." Alice nodded in agreement.

The doctor raised his hand to calm them down. "I don't know much about the disease, but there is probably an incubation period that we have to be aware of. Since it's a virus, I have to do some more research, rather than begin an immediate course of antibiotics, as I would with a bacterial infection of the bowels, for instance. Keep yourselves hydrated and don't let anyone near you. If you want food, tell room service to leave your trays outside your door. I'm going to contact the local authorities in Skagway for instructions and also try to find out from health authorities if there has been any outbreak in the area where you lived. Once I speak with them, I may have to question you again and videotape your replies."

Dr. Benson sat at his computer, trying to concentrate. Coming from the young couple's cabin, his mind had raced, considering the various scenarios. What should he do first? They said that they had worked in West Africa, so he couldn't rule out Ebola. And in Gabon? He had never heard of it. He decided to do a quick Google search to get some basic information on the country.

Apparently, Gabon had been under the control of France for many years, until it gained its independence in 1960. Its population was only about two million, of which about seven hundred thousand lived in the capital city of Libreville, which was on the Atlantic coast. The country had plenty of resources—oil, lumber, and manganese—but with a history of mismanagement and power concentrated in the hands of a few, the disparity between rich and poor was striking. In the rural areas, the villagers lacked basic sanitation and health care, which was probably why Arnie and Alice were sent there in the first place. Apparently there had been a couple of Ebola cases out of Gabon in the mid-nineties. Other West African coastal nations—Liberia, Sierra Leone, Guinea, for instance—had also experienced Ebola outbreaks ever since it had been discovered in 1976 in the Congo.

The doctor then turned his online research to the virus itself. The symptoms appeared to be those being experienced by the young couple: fever, severe headaches, muscle fatigue, diarrhea, vomiting, and abdominal pain.

But, then again, he mused, a patient presenting with severe flu virus also shows those symptoms. He didn't want to be an alarmist, especially with a ship full of guests, but he couldn't rule out the chance that the couple was carrying this dreaded African disease.

He read on. Ebola was spread through direct contact, which in this case was lucky—airborne contagion would have been far more dangerous to the other passengers. Often, the virus got inside the victim's body through the mucous membranes. The doctor found it unsurprising that health care workers in Africa could contract it, particularly if they were working closely on the patient and perhaps not always wearing gloves and a mask. And then, being a married couple, it would have been easy for Alice, say, to have passed along the virus to Arnie in the course of their relations.

He made a note to question the couple closely about contact they'd had with other passengers, particularly Arnie's friends. There would have been hugs in greeting, of course, but they probably wouldn't have shared food, and from their conversation, the doctor felt that they had almost quarantined themselves, needing a toilet close at hand and feeling generally unwell. Armed with very basic information, he picked up his room telephone to call the captain.

Ten minutes later, the captain entered the doctor's cabin and began reviewing the issues at hand.

"This is not good," he started off. "We don't have to alert the passengers at this point yet, as the couple isn't leaving their cabin. Call the Center for Disease Control in Atlanta and ask what we should do. We can always cut short the day at Glacier Bay and head back to Skagway. It might mean delaying our return to Vancouver by a day if the CDC thinks all of the passengers should do blood tests. From what you've shown me online, it looks like there is some kind of test, and if all the other passengers are negative, we can leave the ill couple in Skagway and proceed on our way south. Anyhow, we can hold off on any ship announcement for now. And we are certainly within helicopter range, if the U.S. health authorities want to send out a team to do the testing while we're in transit."

The doctor nodded. "I'll try the CDC first. It's early morning here, so their office will be open. Maybe we can have a game plan in hand before midday. I'll ask the CDC to contact the Alaskan health authorities to coordinate our next steps, and then we can talk to the young couple again."

At this point, Alice and Arnie lay listlessly on their bed, trying to eat a bit of toast and sipping on some tea. Alice had kept the thermometer with them, and found they still registered high fevers. All they could do now was wait for the return of the doctor and wonder what would become of them, although at this point, they were beginning to have difficulty focusing.

An hour or so later, the doctor returned to their cabin. Alice gave him their current temperatures, and he just shook his head. "I've telephoned the CDC and explained your symptoms and the fact that you recently worked in Gabon," he informed them. "I'm told that the CDC will get hold of the health authorities in Gabon to get someone out to the village and the area around it to confirm whether there are any infected people there."

Alice expressed her incredulity that this could be happening. "I know there was an outbreak a few years ago, but I just can't get my head around the possibility that *we're* infected," she cried. "No one warned us about it. And poor Arnie, he's working in a field that should have *no* medical implications, so except for his dumb luck of being married to me, he's facing something totally unexpected." With that, Alice dropped back onto the bed, quietly sobbing.

"We're not saying you have the disease," Dr. Benson said, trying to be comforting. "We're just trying to get a handle on your movements before and during this voyage to determine whether you are a danger to others. And we won't have the information from Gabon immediately. In the meantime, as best you can, go over the interactions you had in the days before you left Gabon, then through your trip to Vancouver, and here on the ship. You and Arnie just remember as much as you can, and I'm going to videotape our interview. We can then email the video to the CDC and the health authorities here in Alaska. It's only mid-morning and people are out enjoying the glaciers. We'll have to make a decision within a few hours whether to keep you both on ship for now and whether to send the ship back to Skagway in quarantine.

"Alice, you're a nurse, so start from the beginning, and Arnie, if you think of something, feel free to jump in. I've got the camera focused so both of your faces are visible, but speak up, if possible."

Alice grimaced. "I hate having my photo taken at the best of times, and I must look awful right now; I've felt too lethargic to use the shower or wash my hair. But if it helps us or anyone else, here goes."

Alice recounted the week of their departure from Gabon, and did confirm, upon reflection, that she hadn't gloved up in helping with the birth of a local child. She remembered that the mother had looked flushed and appeared to be running a fever, but not having been involved in childbirth before—the local midwives were usually called instead of her—she was too overwhelmed to do much of an examination, and put the mother's demeanor down to the rigors of childbirth. The mother had just slept afterward while the local women took the healthy-looking baby to keep it close, awaiting the mother's respite.

"We knew we were headed to Libreville the next day, and everything seemed under control, so I turned my efforts to the patients I had to see before we left," Alice continued. "Arnie planned to come in from the field and join me in the jeep for the ride to the city."

Arnie reached over and patted Alice's shoulder, holding her gently while her sobs renewed.

The doctor shut off the tape recorder for a moment to give Alice a chance to compose herself. "Since you two were together from that time forward, why don't we have Arnie pick up some of the narrative?" he suggested. "Can you remember any physical contact you may have had with others, either in Libreville or on your flight to Canada?" He restarted the tape recorder.

Arnie considered this and replied. "Well, in Libreville we kept pretty much to ourselves. We were beginning our leave from work and it is our first anniversary so . . ." He trailed off for a moment. "On the flight, we'd treated ourselves to business class, so we each had our own pod. Other than service from the steward, we basically slept the whole way, knowing we'd want to have some energy when we met our mates here on the boat."

Alice then joined in. "When we arrived in Vancouver, we had some time to ourselves; Arnie's friends were in the Rockies or thereabouts prior to the cruise. We stayed at a harborside hotel and took a trolley tour around the city, but we didn't really touch anyone, that I can recall. We got on and off the trolley for a couple of hours, but I started feeling queasy, so we went back to the hotel. Arnie began feeling a little unwell the next day, at about the time we boarded, but we put it down to jet lag. It seemed to get worse from there."

The doctor asked them to continue talking about their time on board the ship.

"We boarded around noon," Arnie said, "and still hadn't met up with my mates, but I got a text that they would be along shortly, so we used that time to explore the ship. Walking near the pub, we came upon three women we'd met briefly on the trolley tour, so we chatted with them for a few minutes. We thought about having a beer, but decided to wait until my friends came. Neither of us felt that good, so we went back to our cabin to wait for our luggage. You can see we haven't done much unpacking." Arnie looked ruefully around the room.

The doctor sat forward for a moment. "I meant to ask you before, but forgot—when you were working in Gabon, did you always eat the food you brought, or did the villagers share with you?"

"A bit of both, I think," Arnie answered, after a moment's consideration. "The women cooked really good stews, usually made with chicken, but sometimes with wild boar or antelope—real bushmeat—and sharing in meals was supposed to be part of the experience, so we didn't want to appear standoffish. The stews were often accompanied by yams, rice, or cassava, so our meals were pretty filling. There were also fresh tropical fruits and vegetables. Sometimes, the women brought lunches out to the wells we were working on, and we'd have well water with them. We were trying to show them that the wells were safe and that they should take the trouble to source their water from them, rather than just using streams closer at hand."

"Getting back to your activities after boarding the ship—when did you meet up with your friends?" Dr. Benson asked. "Did you eat with them?"

"Alice met them briefly so that I could introduce her, but she had to beg off because she was feeling kind of nauseated, and since she didn't want any food at that point, I took her back to the room and then rejoined my mates. We were having a few laughs, so we all just grabbed a plate from the buffet near the pool. I ate a burger, but that was it. Alice was able to join us for the quiz later on."

The doctor nodded at Arnie. "Do you recall sharing any of your food or drink with your mates?"

"Why would I do that?" Arnie shot back. "They had their own bloody food and lager is lager! Oh Gawd, my head is killing me!"

Alice patted his arm to settle him down. "The doctor is only trying to help us and the other passengers, Arnie," she said quietly. "If we can give him information about our movements, it may save the cruise line from having to do something drastic." She turned to the doctor. "Doctor, I took a couple of aspirins a while ago. Maybe Arnie should take some more?"

"By all means!" Dr. Benson responded. "I know that this must be awful for you both—looking forward to a special time and coming down with something possibly very dangerous—so we all thank you for your help. Now, other than meeting up with your friends, have you been in contact with anyone else?"

Alice sighed. "The waitstaff brings food and water and leaves it on the table over there, but we haven't had any visitors. Arnie's mates have called and texted, but we told them to stay away because we felt awful, and figured we might be coming down with the flu. The steward offered to change our bedding, but I haven't had the energy to move from the cabin, and in the past day or so Arnie has felt the same way."

"Do you have any medical records with you? I'm thinking like a summary of vaccinations over the last year or so."

Alice sighed again. "I've looked through our luggage, but can't find them. We may have left them in our little office in the village; it was pretty stressful just before we drove to Libreville, so they could be there. And frankly, coming to a first-world country like Canada, vaccination reports weren't the top thing in our minds."

"I'm trying to look at all of the options for you both," the doctor said. "Is it possible that you haven't had typhoid shots?"

Alice looked quizzical. "I have to think we would have had them, but maybe it was some time ago—it wasn't necessary to do them again, was it? I thought the immunity lasted a long time."

The doctor wrung his hands. "It's just a possibility that I want to consider. Once we get someone from the local health authority involved, hopefully they'll test you for that, too. In the meantime, just rest and I'll send this video to CDC and see what steps to take next."

Dr. Benson returned to his office and called the captain. "The young couple isn't doing well. They still have high fevers and the young man is suffering terrible headaches. If this is a flu virus, it's a doozy. I think we should get a hold of the authorities in Skagway and get a helicopter out here to remove them both, using hazmat suits to be on the safe side, with a strict quarantine in place at the local hospital. From the company's perspective, we should also ask that the U.S. authorities get a team ready to meet us in Skagway, with everyone staying on board and submitting blood tests for both Ebola and typhoid fever. If you agree, I'll call the CDC to get their input. The guests aren't going to be happy, but we can still make it to Ketchikan if we cut short the time in Glacier Bay."

Chapter 25

After the women returned from the jazz lounge to their suite, they stepped out onto the veranda. In the late evening, even in summer, it had become a little cool— but glorious all the same, and the night sky showed off the constellations.

Growing up in rural North Dakota, Jean and Olive had both been fascinated by the heavens, able to look at the stars not blurred by any city lights nearby. Maggie hadn't had that opportunity, so she stood next to them quietly, in awe of the spectacle. But Maggie, being Maggie, only muttered, "Boy, do I feel small!" before returning inside to pick out a DVD. She surprised them by choosing *Contact*.

"I wonder if you can get popcorn through room service?" Jean wondered.

The next morning was equally glorious. Arriving at Glacier Bay around seven o'clock, the scene was brilliant—all that sunshine bouncing off the ice surrounding the Bay demanded sunglasses to fully enjoy the show. The radiant heat of the sun countered the cold from the glaciers, so they were able to sit comfortably on the veranda while awaiting their room service breakfast.

Olive began snapping photos, knowing it would be hard to convey the beauty in words to Howard. They agreed that they could move up on deck later on to get a full view.

Hearing a knock at the door, Olive rose to answer it, assuming that room service had arrived.

Instead it was Karen, whispering tentatively. "I hope I didn't disturb you, but Jack is still sleeping and he insists on leaving the drapes to the balcony closed until he is fully awake."

Olive just smiled and motioned for her to come in, while calling to Jean that they had a guest for breakfast. She told Karen that they had ordered room service, but could call and add something for her.

"Thanks so much," Karen whispered again. "Could I have a cheese omelette with toast and coffee?"

Jean had come into the room, so she placed the order. When Karen began to speak again, Jean took her by the arm, chuckling, "You don't have to whisper, you know. Nobody can hear you but us."

Karen grinned sheepishly while making her way out to the veranda.

"Jack and Bev weren't ready to leave the casino last night," she said, "so I came back to the room and looked at all of the stars. It was just so beautiful to see them that clearly. I remember my folks used to take us to a resort upstate when we were kids, and the stars were beautiful then, too—you know, not obscured by city lights. I bet there is a whole generation of children now who don't get to experience that."

Later, another knock sounded at the door. This time it was room service, which also included Karen's breakfast. They all moved inside to eat at the table in the sitting room, enjoying the food in companionable silence.

Karen thought about Jack and how he often talked with his mouth full—it was disgusting, really. He also ate so quickly that he was lighting up one of his dang cigars before she'd finished her meal. This breakfast was wonderful in so many ways.

After setting their empty plates on the service cart, the women all sat back with their coffee.

Olive asked Karen, "So how do you know when you've swallowed something you're allergic to?"

"It varies," Karen responded thoughtfully. "If it's just some peanut oil in the cooking, for instance, I'll feel a tightening in my throat, but often it passes without having to use my EpiPen, although I get it out, just in case. I did have one instance that really scared me. Jack Jr. and I were having lunch at a Thai place in Manhattan, so I told the server I could not tolerate any dish where nuts were involved. Jack Jr. and I both ordered, but somehow the kitchen got my order mixed up with another table's, and since I couldn't see any peanuts in the dish, I didn't think anything of it—and it was really spicy, to boot. It was a noodle dish with chicken, and it tasted great, so I was about four mouthfuls into it before my body reacted. I started to gag, and I guess scared the heck out of my son; I was groping around for my EpiPen, feeling like I was a goner. I did find it, though, and luckily it is fast-acting. The restaurant was very apologetic and gave us our lunch for free, but it sure put a damper on our outing in Manhattan. To this day, Jack Jr. keeps apologizing, but I've told him it wasn't his fault; it was a mix-up in the kitchen."

The women just stared at Karen, trying to imagine themselves in that predicament.

Maggie picked up her coffee and moved toward the veranda. "Let's watch from here for a little while and then head up to the observation deck," she said. "There may be a lot of people up there, but that can be part of the fun, watching others' reactions. Karen, at some point you'll probably want to put on some heavier clothing, but you're welcome to join us for the day.

Although if Jack surprises you and wants to spend the day with you, we'll understand."

Olive welcomed an opportunity to walk around the outer deck a few times in an effort to counteract the calories lying in wait at the gala dinner that night. Seeing Glacier Bay from the observation deck was beautiful, and, as Maggie had predicted, the people-watching was almost as interesting as the glaciers.

As they were turning to walk inside, Jean pointed to the sky, and soon they heard the unmistakable whir of helicopter blades. After a helicopter landed on the helipad at the end of the ship, the noise subsided, and the women and other interested spectators leaned over the deck for a better view of the commotion. Alighting from the chopper were three figures wearing heavy protective suits, like in the movies.

The women gaped at each other. Since it was warm in the sunshine, they decided to hold off on returning to their suite for the time being.

Twenty minutes later, the figures reappeared from below deck, carrying a stretcher bearing what appeared to be a person, also covered in protective gear. Depositing the stretcher into the helicopter, the figures returned inside the ship, bearing another empty stretcher. On their walk back to the helicopter, they carried the stretcher, which at this time was occupied by another person covered in protective gear.

The crowd around the women murmured, obviously wondering if there was some kind of emergency. Then the helicopter flew off, so the women and some of the crowd strolled inside.

In the afternoon, they decided to change venues, and settled into some reclining chairs between the hot tubs and the pool, enjoying the opportunity to read or do crossword puzzles.

No sooner had Olive commented that Jack must have agreed to glacier-watch with Karen, that they heard his booming voice: "Get off my back, will you! I watched it with you, didn't I? So the glaciers are smaller than they used to be. Boo hoo! It still looks like there are a lot of them left, as far as I can see!" Jack and Karen approached where the women were sitting. "Here, you can sit with the women while I go for a smoke. I'll come back for a soak in the hot tub after. Bev says she might join us at some point."

The women focused on their books so as not to witness Karen's embarrassment. She astutely noticed them not noticing, and laughed ruefully as soon as Jack waddled away. "Don't worry, gals. I'm used to this. He'll take the burr out of his paw, have his smoke, and then be civil again."

Olive looked up. "Jack said Bev will probably come down to the pool later. How is she doing? Is her son planning on meeting her in Vancouver?"

Karen shook her head. "The woman is a marvel. As they say in the old movies, she's bearing up remarkably well. Jack talked Matt out of coming all this way to meet her, and Bev will just fly back with us, so he can pick her up at the airport in New York. No word on the body as of this morning, though. At some point they'll either do an autopsy or cremate Art, I guess."

Jack arrived again about thirty minutes later, deep in conversation, it appeared, with a like-minded individual, also with a booming voice, but with a Southern drawl. The men both entered the hot tub, but luckily, they were facing the port side of the ship, so the women were able to continue reading without too much interruption.

Olive told Jean that she had to use the bathroom and asked if she would she like a snack of some sorts. A thumbs up from Jean had Olive in search of the table adjacent to the buffet area, which usually held little cakes and savory snacks in the afternoon. She had just rounded the hallway when she noticed Bev standing at the end of the table, gesturing to someone Olive could not see due to a wall blocking her view.

Bev was obviously upset at her listener, as her lips were pursed and she was waving her hands in the air. Although Olive was curious, she didn't want to accost Bev and interrupt the conversation.

After picking up a couple of bags of potato chips, she strode back toward Jean and the others. A little while later, Bev made an appearance, and although she nodded to Karen and the other women, she quickly joined Jack and his new-found friend in the hot tub. Olive couldn't help but reflect that grief must take many forms.

Just then, their attention was drawn by an announcement from the ship's captain. This time, unfortunately, it did not involve any whale sighting. "Attention, please," his voice boomed out from the speakers above the pool. "We regret that, due to a medical emergency, we must cut our Glacier Bay visit short and return to Skagway. Two ill passengers have been removed from the ship by helicopter, and will be held in quarantine in Skagway until the precise nature of their illness has been confirmed. In Skagway, a medical team will board the ship to draw blood from all passengers and crew, so that we can then get underway to Ketchikan, our next port of call. We have done a thorough investigation of the movements of the two passengers and feel confident that none of you are in danger; however, we want to be sure by having blood taken for testing. All passengers and crew will remain on the ship during the testing period. We will keep you apprised of any developments."

As with the sighting of the helicopter and removal of the two passengers, the announcement drew some murmuring questions and shaking of heads from the remaining passengers. To date, the cruise had been so effortless and pampering that most passengers appeared not to be too alarmed, and went about their activities as usual.

Olive marveled at the captain's equanimity. The poor fellow was obviously dealing with something bad enough to warrant a return to Skagway, and was still supposed to be calm and charming at the Captain's dinner that evening.

Chapter 26

The dining room positively glittered! It truly was a gala evening, and the women felt quite sophisticated in their long skirts and blouses.

Looking across the dining room, Olive saw that Jack had invited the fellow from the hot tub and his wife to join him, as well as Bev and Karen. Since Olive could see them from their own table, she nudged Jean to point out that Jack's behavior was the same as on the first night of the cruise. He, the other fellow, and Bev were locked in a conversation of their own, while Karen and the other wife sat in comparative silence. Olive shook her head. While she was sad about Karen's situation, she wasn't going to let it affect her own evening.

Continuing to survey the room, Olive spotted the Countess and her companion at the entrance. She waved them to a table for two next to theirs, watching the Countess smile in response.

The server had come back with their cocktails, so she asked him to remain for a moment, in case the Countess also wanted a beverage. Before the Countess took her seat, Maggie asked if she could take a photo of them at their table, realizing that they had none to show Howard. In response, the Countess motioned to her companion, who took a couple of photos for the women to choose from.

The women sat back in appreciation of their surroundings. Even the Countess appeared to be enjoying herself, exchanging pleasantries with Olive. And the menu! As always, there was something for everyone's taste, even innovative vegetarian dishes. The trio had eaten nothing since breakfast, wanting to try the soup *and* the starters *and* the entrées *and* the desserts.

"If I'm going down, I'm going down in style," Jean exclaimed. "Look at these soups! *Pasta e fagioli*—kinda looks like Italian wedding soup, but then the roasted parsnip—that's probably right up Olive's alley. And the starters! Maggie, I'll bet you'll try the mushroom crostini or the pineapple jumbo shrimp with Thai dipping sauce, and Olive's going to be all over the foie gras with rhubarb compote, for sure. Am I right?"

Jean's voice carried, as always; both the Countess and her companion looked on quizzically, while Maggie and Olive broke out in gales of laughter. Jean would never make a good spy.

Maggie spoke up next. "I can't believe the entrées! Steamed Alaskan crab, boneless lamb *en croute*, whatever that is, basil-crusted pork rack with morels, and for the beef lover in all of us, cracked pepper tenderloin with grilled shrimp."

Back to Jean. "And don't get me going on the desserts! Tiramisu, lemon meringue cheesecake, black forest cake. I'm glad we did our little walk today . . . but let's order dessert for room service later. There's no way I can take it all in at one sitting."

The women still had some wine left from an earlier dinner, and began sipping on the cocktails the server had already delivered. In further conversation between the two tables, the Countess mentioned that she was considering the tour of Ketchikan the next day, as it appeared the tour did not involve a lot of walking; she had always admired the skill of the Natives in creating their massive totem poles.

When the food began to arrive, the women all smiled and turned to their own conversation. The Countess and her companion ate in silence.

While waiting for coffee to be served, the Countess leaned over toward Olive. "At our first dinner here, I noticed that there was another man at the table with the loud American man, and that all three of you were also at the table. Are you all friends?"

Olive looked back at her in surprise. "Well, actually, we're not really friends," she replied. "We met the two couples in Vancouver prior to boarding and became friends with Jack's wife, Karen, whom you met in Skagway, and Art, the fellow you're inquiring about. Unfortunately, Art died of apparently natural causes during his hike outside of Skagway, although his death is still being investigated."

The Countess frowned. "And that woman sitting across from 'Jack' is Art's widow? Forgive me for saying this, but she does not look overwhelmed with grief."

Olive could only respond, "No, she doesn't."

Maggie looked over at Karen's table, noting that nothing much had changed. Jack and his new friend were laughing hard at something while Karen looked on impassively. Maggie had been bitter at first about her ex-husband, the philandering S.O.B., but they had shared a lot of good times, too, and, of course, had produced their wonderful daughter together. She couldn't imagine sitting next to a man for that many years and playing such a small part in his life. *It must just be killing Karen,* Maggie thought. It would sure be killing her.

Later, as the trio began leaving the dining room, Karen rose from her seat and walked over to them. "Any chance I can join you in the pub for the quiz?" she asked.

The women answered "Yes!" in unison, bringing a grateful grin in return.

Entering the pub later on, they spied the two Australians, who began waving them over. One of them shouted above the din, "Didya hear about our mate and his wife? They've been taken off the boat. They're pretty sick, I guess, but in these modern times, for Gawd's sake, the hospital in Skagway should have something for them, don't ya think? They hardly had a chance to do anything since they got on board, poor devils! And then we all had to get blood tests—but that made sense, so we're not going to worry about it."

The questions that night included some about sports and songs from the early Sixties—right up Maggie's alley—so their team took the prize. Not wanting to turn in just yet, the group decided to stay at the pub for the acoustic musician-slash-singer and weren't disappointed. His repertoire included many of their favorites from the Sixties and Seventies. A lot of the crowd sang along. Knowing that Jack and Bev would be hunched over the gaming tables in the casino, Karen appreciated the camaraderie in the pub all the more.

At the end of the performer's set, Maggie stood up. "I didn't realize that doing nothing all day could take so much out of me!" she exclaimed. "Looks like tomorrow in Ketchikan will be interesting. I'm heading back to the suite." Jean nodded in agreement.

Olive looked over at Karen, who was staring into the middle distance. "It sounds like the jazz group next door is just starting. If you want to join me, Karen, we can have a nightcap and listen to the first set," she offered.

Karen nodded, smiling. "That would be great!"

Chapter 27

The Countess had wanted another cup of coffee, so she'd declined the women's offer to join them in the pub. Across from her, she could see Annie fidget. Well, let her fidget! She probably just wanted to skulk off to see her new friend. *She should probably give Annie a little more freedom on this trip*, she thought, knowing that her little sparrow's gratitude would remain for weeks. Perhaps she would go on that tour in Ketchikan tomorrow, allowing Annie time to meet up with her man. No doubt she would pour out all of her troubles to him.

The Countess' mind turned to the other diners. Olive, Jean, and Maggie, it appeared, like so many North Americans, always had to be *doing* something, so they could regale friends and family with remembrances and photos, usually of themselves in some new setting. What could be the fun in a "quiz," for instance? A roomful of people drinking beer and struggling to answer questions for some little prize?

On the Countess' honeymoon, all the passengers enjoyed chamber music, bridge, and after-dinner strolls on the promenade deck, perhaps returning to the lounge for a cognac and conversation. It being just after World War II, she recalled how people had asked her late husband about Germany, after he had assured them, of course, that he had never had any use for Hitler. He'd told them wistfully of the Bavaria he remembered as a child, and that, while he missed it, he appreciated the future that Alaska and Canada had to offer. Many of their fellow passengers, American and Canadian alike, had nodded gravely, murmuring "Here, here."

The Countess enjoyed her conversations with Olive, who hadn't provided a lot of information about herself, save for the loss of her husband, but appeared content to mostly listen. Her sister, Jean—the one with flaming red hair—on the other hand, was almost as noisy as that American man holding court at the table where the dead fellow, Art, used to sit. She could just picture Jean right now, dominating the quiz team, although, upon reflection, she might have some competition with the other woman, Maggie, for volume.

And this "Art" person, dying all by himself on some hiking trail in Alaska. The thought made the Countess shudder, remembering the death of her husband and son, wondering what Willie's last thoughts would have been, as he frantically tried to save his father. And where was Art's wife while this was going on? Her cheerfulness was actually chilling to the Countess, again remembering her unbridled grief when learning of the deaths of Heinz and Willie.

When I die I want to be peacefully asleep, and never wake up, she thought.

She inspected Annie, sitting across from her, gazing back at her impassively. *Like she would care if I died!* The Countess thought. *The silverware would be gone before Annie called the police.*

An had begun to feel uncomfortable. Sometimes she feared that the Countess could read her thoughts. She wanted to flee the table, to meet with Li-Liang and discuss her path to freedom. She had given him her room key, making sure that the Countess had hers when they left the room. If her "loss" of the key had been discovered, she could just pretend to be "that stupid girl" until it miraculously appeared again. Luckily, it wouldn't be an issue.

The Countess appeared to be staring at her, but An knew that it wasn't necessarily so. She had learned that when her employer stared like that, An became like the "middle distance" to her, not an actual person who might be an object to stare at.

What was the Countess thinking about tonight? It was obviously not a pleasant thought, because her temples were twitching.

Li-Liang moved quickly around the Countess' suite. Timing was critical, he realized, knowing that the stewards went from room to room while the passengers were at dinner or some other entertainment, using the half-hour or so to turn down the beds and remove any room service trays. Finding a stranger in the suite would raise an alarm, an alarm that he would not be able to explain, and which would put An's employment in jeopardy.

He used a small flashlight to guide his way, not wanting a steward to open the door and inquire about one thing or another of the Countess. There were three suitcases in the closet. Dang, he should have gotten more specifics from An. But luckily, lifting each one answered his question; the contents of two of them had obviously been emptied into drawers, while the third still had some weight. He lifted it onto the bed, praying that it was unlocked.

No such luck! Looking at his watch, he began going through each drawer, wishing that the Countess had put the key in her underwear drawer, like in the movies. Going through an old woman's underwear would not be the high point of his evening, he thought ruefully, but what must be done, must be done.

He continued his search, rifling through all of the drawers, noting that An's underthings were much more interesting, but found nothing. The Countess probably kept the key on her person or in her handbag. When he met up with An later this evening, he would have to get her to agree to do a more thorough search herself when her mistress left the suite.

Li-Liang could wait no longer. Peering out into the hallway and seeing no one approach, he left An's key on the small table next to the door inside her suite and crept down to the elevator.

The Countess finished her coffee and rose from the table, peering down at her servant. "Annie, you can take me to the suite and then leave me to rest. If you want, you can spend the rest of the evening on your own—or, I suspect, meeting up with your new *boyfriend*," she sneered, knowing that the term bothered Annie.

When they arrived at the suite, the Countess told Annie to open the door. Annie stuttered, searching in her pocket long enough that the Countess sighed and took out her own key, letting them into the room.

"You are no help to me if you are forgetful!" she barked at Annie, and pointed to the key on the table near the door.

"Yes, Madame," was all the girl could muster.

"Alright, then, go along with you, but take your key!" the Countess snapped. "I don't want to have to get out of bed just to let you back in."

After Annie left, the Countess opened the closet and retrieved her suitcase. She removed the key from her cosmetic bag in the bathroom and opened the suitcase.

Something was bothering her, she realized as she handled the gowns. A faint odor of cologne hung in the air, and the suitcase had been somewhat askew in the closet. *Probably one of the stewards*, she thought. Yet, that was strange—it was the first time she had noticed that smell.

Chapter 28

"The time on this cruise has passed so quickly!" Jean exclaimed, looking out the veranda door. "Some know-it-all at Flushing Meadows told me we'd find it really boring, although when I asked her what cruises she had tried, she didn't have an answer. I can't believe that this is the last port of call in Alaska. And it's good that Olive has some great photos to show Howard."

Olive smiled, feeling a tingle of anticipation in thinking about seeing Howard again.

The detour back to Skagway had been handled efficiently, with a team waiting for them with kits to take everyone's blood. The team had started with the staff so that they could get on with their duties. Some passengers had waited in their cabins or on deck, waiting to be called by their order on the passenger list.

Olive had sighted a uniformed State trooper and what appeared to be a plainclothes detective walk up from shore and speak to the ship's doctor. Since the detective held Art's backpack in his hand, Olive quietly strode near them, hoping to overhear their conversation.

She'd heard the doctor say, "I believe Mrs. Herrington is in her cabin waiting for her blood test. Do you want to speak to her? I can deliver her husband's clothing and backpack to her, if you wish."

"Sure," the detective had replied. "Just tell her that the coroner does plan to do the autopsy today, if possible. The fact that the other hikers saw Mr. Herrington quite healthy just before his death seems reason enough to investigate the cause of death. The coroner kept an inventory of his backpack, so we no longer need to retain it. I've been asked to remain on board as far as Ketchikan in case any further information is required from Mrs. Herrington. I'll also be available if any passengers have questions about the blood test results."

"I'd sure like to look inside the backpack, although if Art ate the sandwich, there will be nothing to go on anyway," Olive had murmured to herself.

Jean's loud bark called Olive back to the present. "And today we go on that tour to the park with all the totem poles and Native crafts," she said. "It should be really interesting."

Maggie looked over at Olive. "So, did Karen have any further information about Art last night?"

"No, I guess. Or at least she didn't volunteer any, and I didn't think to ask her," Olive replied. "She did say that Jack agreed to come on one of the totem tours today, as we're in port until seven o'clock. They plan to sleep in, have lunch in their suite, and then take a later tour. So that's good, them doing something together."

Jean asked Maggie, "Which tour do you want to take? I agree with Olive that it might be better to take an earlier tour and then spend the afternoon by the pool, like yesterday. Aside from the blood tests, that was certainly relaxing."

Maggie saluted. "I'm on board, Captain!" she said, giggling at the groans of her shipmates.

They knew they could enjoy a leisurely breakfast, and even though the ship wasn't docking until noon—a little later than anticipated due to the detour back to Skagway—they could still take the two-hour tour and be back on the ship for a late lunch or a mid-afternoon poolside snack if they wanted one. Ah, this was the life!

Again, it amazed them all to watch the pilot dock the ship—so smooth, with such precision! They looked shoreside and saw numerous shops and kiosks waiting for their business. This would be their last chance to buy souvenirs in Alaska.

"I'm trying to think of something Jon and Karen would like that's authentic and tasteful," Olive said. "Howard and I intend to visit them in October, after the harvest, and it would be great to take them something for the house, and maybe something to wear, too, like those wool caps for winter."

Jean nodded to Olive. "Yes, that's a great idea. I want to get them something, too. Maybe a scarf for Karen and some mittens for Jon. But I don't want to load you and Howard down for the plane trip to North Dakota. I also want to buy a scarf, and maybe some hand-crafted earrings for Chantelle."

Maggie laughed. "Gee, if you do all that, I won't have to buy my daughter anything!" she said, knowing full well that she also planned to buy a souvenir for her. "We might want to get a print for the apartment, too!"

As the women stepped off the gangplank, Olive looked around and sighed. "We really have been blessed with good weather. The trip out to the historic site apparently takes us where we have a good view of the town and the water. The brochure in the suite says there is a traditional clan house at the site as well."

Turning toward the small bus pulling up to the wharf, Olive heard a voice calling her name. She motioned Jean and Maggie to stop for a moment while she walked back to the Countess, who had been calling her.

"I've decided to take the tour after all," the Countess announced. She gave Olive a peck on the cheek and then strode toward the others, offering them a slight wave of greeting. "The brochure in my suite provided a good description, especially of the clan house. My late husband became friendly with the Natives when he was panning for gold, and a number of times he purchased a homemade mask or a woven bowl to bring home."

As with each shore excursion before it, the trip around Ketchikan offered a wonderful narrative, this time by a young fellow who described his people as Tlingit. Olive had already learned that west coast Natives had begun referring to themselves as "First Nation," which made sense for sure, and the group was comprised of a number of subgroups: Haida, Tlingit, Tsimshian, and further south, the Coast Salish. The guide explained that the totem poles were hand-carved and represented the five clans of the coast people, known respectively as Raven, Eagle, Frog, Wolf and Split-Tail Beaver. The poles were tall and intricately carved. A huge dugout canoe was also on exhibit.

The building at the Totem Heritage Center had black-and-white photos showing Native men in conical hats made of cedar strips paddling the huge dugout boats. Apparently, they'd fished from them, and at times conducted raids on other tribes. The men looked very muscular and rather fierce. Olive could see that only the guns and cannons of the white explorers had allowed them to prevail. Unfortunately, the white men brought not only guns, but smallpox, to these coastal people, wiping out a large percentage of them in a short space of time.

Pointing out the photos to Jean, Olive sighed. "This is progress?"

While the Countess had been friendly and communicative on the bus, she wandered off in the clan house, clearly interested in the exhibits, perhaps remembering the summers past. She picked up a couple of items, then put them down, shaking her head.

Back at the dock, with the tour over, the Countess bade the trio goodbye, telling them that she was looking forward to cup of coffee on board the ship.

Maggie suggested to the other women that they finish their shopping before returning to their suite. "It's still early, so we've got plenty of time. Olive, you and Jean lucked out in the gift shop at the Heritage Center—Jon and Karen will love that Raven-themed table runner and napkins, and Jean, Chantelle is going to freak out over the hammered silver earrings. You really shouldn't have!"

They wandered into a huge store right by the dock, and Maggie went in search of a wool cap and mittens for Chantelle, while Jean and Olive looked through Native prints to take some home for framing. The art was so distinctive, and they could just visualize the perfect place for them. Jean picked out a couple to show Maggie, so that they could decide together. Olive felt sure that the one she chose would please Howard. She'd wait until they returned to Vancouver to buy his Cowichan sweater.

Chapter 29

An was very happy that the Countess had decided to take the tour, giving her the opportunity to let Li-Liang into the suite to help her search for the suitcase key. And if a steward stopped by, so what? She occupied the suite, too, and if she wanted to invite a guest to join her, it should raise no suspicions. But it was imperative that he be out of the room before the Countess returned.

An heard a slight tap at the door and her heart quickened. Seeing Li-Liang's grin put it in full flutter. She enjoyed his attention and didn't want the cruise to end. He had said nothing about the future, but surely he was sincere?

Entering the room and closing the door quickly, he was all business, first bringing the suitcase to the bed and then motioning her to help him go around the room again in search of the key.

"Could the old woman have put the key around her neck?" he asked.

An shook her head. "She wears a nightgown, but it is open at the neck and there was no necklace or chain there."

"What about her handbag?" Li-Liang was clearly losing patience.

"I looked there when she was in the bathroom this morning, and it is not there."

"Where have you yet to look?" Li-Liang motioned around the suite.

"She just left, and I wanted to make sure that she was not returning, so I decided to wait until you arrived.

The bus should have left by now," An said. "She often keeps her cosmetic bag in the table next to her bed, but I didn't see it there, so I planned to thoroughly check all containers in the bathroom."

An moved toward the bathroom door while Li-Liang decided to try the suitcase once more. He looked up, startled, upon hearing the girl squeal.

She walked quickly toward him. "The Countess left her cosmetic bag in the bathroom this morning, and this was in it!" Pointing to the key, she handed it off to Li-Liang, who immediately thrust it into the case, opening the lid to reveal its contents.

He began to rage. "It's just a couple of old gowns, for God's sake! I thought you said she might be receiving gold, or maybe even jewels from her relative. You got me involved for nothing!"

An was distraught, and removed one of the gowns in disbelief, tears forming in her eyes.

Li-Liang grabbed it from her in anger, then stopped, moving the gown from one hand to another, feeling the weight. He then put it down on the bed and began feeling the hem and bodice. "My God, the old girl has stones sewn into these garments. How clever!" he exclaimed. "Stop crying, An. I'm sorry I yelled at you. Let's decide upon a plan before your mistress returns."

The Countess slowly walked up the gangplank, reflecting on the creativity of the Native artists, and the enjoyment she felt in watching Olive and the others appreciate the artistry. She had almost bought one of the beautiful scarves herself, but what was the use? Had Heinz seen it, he would have bought it for her, lovingly draping it over her neck. Well, she had clothes and accessories she hadn't worn in years, so why add to the list?

But then she had to chuckle ruefully about the old

gowns and the good use she was finding for them. This brought a spring to her step as she made her way back to the suite.

When she got there, the rooms were empty. Annie was nowhere to be found, and there was that faint smell of cologne again. It could have been worn by the same steward—but then, what if Annie had invited that stranger in for a visit? No, that couldn't be, as the fragrance was there the other day, too, when both she and Annie had been out. Ah, but Annie had also left her key in the suite, hadn't she?

The Countess resolved to talk to her tonight and get at the truth. She hastily checked the closet, satisfied that the suitcase was still there.

All of these suspicious thoughts made her feel alone, and she didn't like it. Perhaps some coffee from room service and a light lunch might make her feel better? No, she did not feel like remaining in the room; she would go to the public area near the pool, and if she encountered Olive, she could admire her purchases.

Stepping out of her suite, she looked down the hallway to see the big American fellow, followed by a steward, and Olive, of all people, walking quickly toward one of the staterooms, all with worried expressions.

Chapter 30

Walking back onto the ship, Jean had suggested they stop by the pool area to see whether it was crowded. As they entered the Lido lounge, Jack strode towards them, all smiles. "So, ladies, how was the tour? Karen and I are getting some room service lunch and, if you recommend it, we'll take the later tour."

The women exchanged glances. What was this all about? He was Mr. Nice guy all of a sudden.

Maybe he's glad the cruise is almost over? Olive wondered.

Maggie answered his question. "The tour is really something. The totem poles are beautiful and the history is fascinating. Bev would probably like it, too."

Jack favored them with another big smile. "Haven't seen Bev today. Art's death is probably starting to sink in, poor girl. We'll check in on her later," he said. "Well, I'm off. Karen told me she feels like something spicy to go with a cold beer, so we'll see what that's all about." Another big smile.

Jean just muttered "Jeez" at Jack's departure. "If he would do that around Karen, she'd probably feel a lot better."

"Oh, good—looks like there's a lot of room by the pool, so let's change and we can order something to eat and drink when we come back," Maggie said, gently pushing Olive and Jean toward the elevators. Then she ran back and quickly put three towels on chairs next to each other, while Olive laughed.

"Our very own tour director!" Olive chuckled.

The women had just settled into the chairs and were enjoying nachos and beer when Jack walked toward them. "Karen and I were going to start lunch, but I realized I left my phone down here. Not sure where, but I hope someone has turned it in," he said.

He walked past them to a couple of chairs next to a table on the other side of the pool and appeared to rummage around under them. He then stood up, smiled broadly, and, holding the phone in his hand, strode back toward them. "Whew! That's a relief. Don't know what I was thinking about."

Surprised, the women listened as he continued. They'd heard more friendly sentences from him in the past thirty minutes than the days before combined.

"Karen is happy that room service is able to serve up Thai food. We're both having this noodle dish with chicken," he told them.

"Isn't she really allergic to nuts?" Olive was skeptical. "What if there's a misunderstanding in the kitchen?"

Jack just waved her off. "I heard her order and she was really specific, so I suppose they'll mark her dish different from mine, so there should be no problem. I'm going back up anyway to eat lunch."

As Jack got on the elevator, he had to stifle a grin. People were so gullible. Poor Karen, anaphylaxis was *not* a good way to go. At least that's what he'd been told a couple of years earlier, when she'd had her attack while eating with their son; Jack Jr. had been badly shaken by it.

When Jack ordered the room service, he had, in fact, ordered a nut-free version, but that wasn't what Karen ate. With his help, gently but forcibly feeding her some of the dish, her eyes wide in terror, he'd waited while she started to convulse. She couldn't even speak, but kept trying to reach for her EpiPen, which he made sure was beyond her reach. Jack left her struggling to breathe, knowing that the end was near, but wanting to meet up with anyone who could testify to his whereabouts.

He couldn't believe his luck when he saw that the women were still by the pool. He could tell them about the lunch that he should "get back to," now that he'd found his phone. And they had listened to all of his story before he rode the elevator back to his suite.

Now, at the door, he gently let himself in and checked on Karen, slumped at the table and very, very still. He didn't want to touch her, so he knelt down to listen for her breathing; he couldn't hear anything. Using a washcloth from the bathroom, he carefully moved the EpiPen further out of her reach. Leaving his key on the bedside table, he hurried back down to the pool area, ostensibly in search of a steward to let him back into the suite, but more importantly, to fix his time outside the room for anyone interested.

The women looked up at the sound of Jack's voice. "Where can I find a steward?" he asked. "I left my key when I came down to look for my phone, but when I knocked on the door of the suite and called out to Karen, no one answered!"

Olive ventured, "Maybe she's in the bathroom?"

"I waited a couple of minutes or so!" Jack answered in a panicked tone.

Jean took out her phone. "Karen and I exchanged telephone numbers. I'll try to get hold of her." She dialed and heard the phone ring, but then it went to voicemail. "No answer."

In response, Jack knocked himself in the forehead, saying that he should have thought of that. He took out his phone and contacted Bev, who apparently was in her suite. No, Karen wasn't there either. The women gathered up their belongings and followed Jack to the elevator, calling out to a server that a steward with a key was required at Jack's suite.

The steward opened the door to Jack's suite. The women walked in behind Jack as he called out, "Karen, Karen?"

They all stopped abruptly as they sighted Karen's body slumped over the table, which held her partly eaten lunch and Jack's untouched plate. He bent over her, felt for a pulse, and then started to weep.

Olive supposed that they should all just leave, but to her mind, Karen's demise was too coincidental to ignore. Walking around the steward, she was able to get a better look at Karen, and the sight was disturbing, to say the least.

It appeared that Karen had tried to reach for her EpiPen, which was off to the side on a table next to the couch, enough beyond her reach that she would have had to stand to reach it. The allergy attack must have been sudden and severe, as Karen appeared to have held tightly to the table before falling into it, rather than slumping to the floor. Jack was weeping vociferously now, but again, Olive couldn't bring herself to believe that this was all an accident.

After a few minutes of uncontrollable sobbing, Jack called Bev on his phone. When she inevitably entered the suite, she looked appropriately surprised, rushing to Jack's side saying, "Jackie, Jackie," which seemed to Olive to be a little intimate, given the circumstances.

Olive ventured her condolences, while asking, "Do you think the kitchen sent up the wrong lunch for Karen? You should get the food tested to confirm the contents on her plate, and your lunch, too. If they mixed up the order, I'm sure the cruise line should try to make amends. You can't bring Karen back, but shouldn't something come of this?"

While Jack looked on, she told the steward that he should contact one of his superiors to ask what must be done. Jack's tears had dried and he appeared to eye Olive warily while she talked to the steward.

"I'm not sure if that's necessary," he said. "You're right; we can't bring Karen back."

As the steward left the suite, Maggie and Jean glanced at each other with raised eyebrows. They were still voicing their condolences as Olive left the room to follow the steward. Then they walked toward their own suite, not knowing that Olive had taken the elevator *with* the steward until they entered their suite and found it empty. After realizing what her sister had done, Jean groaned. "Christ on a bicycle! I hope she's not going to get in the middle of this."

Back in the suite, Jack and Bev stared at Karen's body for a few minutes. Bev put her head on Jack's chest. "I can't believe what has happened. It's all so strange." Had she been looking into Jack's face she would have seen the trace of a smile.

Olive followed the steward into the chief steward's office. He looked up quizzically, so she launched into her narrative, ending with her suspicions about the coincidental deaths of Art and Karen. Since Art's death had occurred on land, the cruise line, while making a note of it, would not have made the connection that Olive was trying to explain. She asked whether Jack's suite could be sealed until the police had the opportunity to search it.

"Madame, if I may," the chief steward said as he gestured to the other steward to find the captain, "are you a relative?"

"Well, no," Olive admitted. "My sister, a friend, and I have gotten to know Karen—as we had also gotten to know Art—and frankly, we think there should at least be an investigation. We don't know what the Skagway police concluded, or whether an autopsy was ordered for Art, but again, this all seems too coincidental to dismiss as just a couple of unrelated deaths."

"So you think there might be foul play?" the steward asked, unimpressed. "Who would you consider a suspect?"

Olive answered hesitantly. "I don't want to stick my neck into a possible lawsuit from Karen's husband, so I'll say this in confidence. In observing Jack Leonard's behavior since meeting him, he seemed to have little to do with Karen, preferring the company of Art Herrington's wife, Beverly. In Skagway, as we were all leaving the ship on our excursions, I noticed him putting food in Art Herrington's backpack. Art died on the way down from his hike. Jack and Bev were conveniently golfing at the time. I don't think that Bev is complicit, but this turn of events certainly makes their future together more cozy."

At that moment, the captain entered the chief steward's office. "We just had a death on board?" he demanded. "We're set to leave in about a couple of hours or so. The steward told me it looked like the woman had a severe allergic reaction to some food and couldn't reach her medicine. Is that right?"

Olive spoke up. "I've been in the suite and she is dead. Her husband, Jack Leonard, is still with her, I believe."

"Madame, if I may . . ." the captain began.

"No, I'm not a relative," Olive sighed. "I have told the chief steward all that I know and I'm concerned that the victim's husband will clear away any evidence of foul play. But this would be the time to check his suite for any substance which might have hastened Art's death."

"Who is 'Art?'" asked the captain.

Olive sighed and gave a truncated account of Art Herrington's death to the captain, concerned that inaction would play into Jack's hands.

The captain nodded. "Since the death occurred on board, we can contact the State police to investigate, especially since the husband is alleging that our negligence caused his wife's death. In fact, I'll do it right now," he said, but he obviously meant after Olive left. "Since it *is* a possible crime scene, I think the police will be able to thoroughly search the suite without a search warrant. I suggest that you go back to your suite for now, and feel free, of course, to go to dinner as well. We have your suite number." He paused. "By the way, I'm curious. Why do you think that Mr. Herrington was poisoned? And with what? It seems a little farfetched."

"I'm not an alarmist, but when Art died so suddenly, particularly as he was taking medication and with the Skagway officer telling us that the hike wasn't so strenuous, I just had a bad feeling," Olive responded. "So I did some research and apparently aconite, as it's called, is readily available and can be added to spicy food without the victim knowing. Jack and Karen live just outside Manhattan, which has a large Chinatown, and I'll bet Jack could buy what he needed from a herbalist. I don't want to accuse him without evidence, but it's worth looking into—without mentioning me, of course."

Chapter 31

Olive couldn't avoid the accusatory stares as she let herself into the suite.

"Okay, Sherlock, what have you found out?" Jean asked, wagging her finger at Olive.

"All I've done is set out my concerns to the captain and he said he'll take it from here," Olive responded calmly. "He's contacting the State police. I assume the chief steward will speak to the detective who boarded the ship in Skagway; no doubt he will be looking into Karen's death at the request of the cruise line. I imagine the ship is trying to stay as close to schedule as possible, as people probably have planes to catch in Vancouver."

"Us being three of those people, Olive." Maggie grinned ruefully. "Well, with all of this excitement and with only a day or so left on board, I'm ready to enjoy some of that scotch Howard bought for our suite. And I'm not missing dinner either! No doubt Jack and Bev can console each other without our help . . ."

Unbeknownst to Maggie or Jean, Olive had left their door ajar in hopes of hearing whether any police would, in fact, board the ship and search Jack's suite, just down the hallway from theirs. Since it was late afternoon and the sun hadn't sunk into dusk, Maggie and Jean took their drinks onto the veranda, while Olive stood in the middle of the suite, listening for any footsteps in the hall.

About twenty minutes later, she heard sounds outside their door and looked out to see an armed officer and a man in a suit knock on Jack's door. She could hear Jack's voice, loud as it was, asking, "What is this all about?" She could hear the murmur of a response, and Jack then shouting, "Don't you people have any decency? I just lost my wife to her allergy problem, for God's sake! What are you doing, looking through our suite?"

She then saw the uniformed officer escort Jack and Bev from his suite, Jack red in the face and very angry, and Bev looking confused. The officer told him to wait someplace comfortable, that this was standard procedure when a death occurred, and that they would question him later.

She heard Jack say, "Alright then, I'll wait in our friend's suite next door. I have to call our son about this, anyway."

At that moment, Jack looked down the hall to see Olive staring at the group and his eyes narrowed. Olive slipped back into her suite, feeling like a voyeur, but also a little apprehensive about Jack's expression. She hoped he wouldn't find out that she had instigated the investigation.

Maggie called out, "Olive, where are you? The breeze is wonderful out here. And bring that bag of peanuts with you."

Jean noticed that Olive looked a little pale when she took her seat beside the other women. "What's up, kiddo?" she asked.

Olive replied, "I was watching the police enter Jack's suite and could hear him shouting. He obviously doesn't want any investigation, so I hope the captain doesn't mention me. The police obviously shooed him out of the suite, so I saw him in the hall on his way to Bev's suite. But he turned toward me and gave me the most venomous look before I could slip back in here. It was really unnerving."

Maggie exchanged glances with Jean. "Alright, concerned citizen," she said. "You've done your bit. The police will take charge and do whatever, but your job now is to forget about all of this and enjoy our evening aboard ship. We're going to dine, do the quiz, and listen to jazz, just like we've done since we boarded. And tomorrow we're going back down the Inside Passage, and since we'll be looking out at the other shoreline, we should get a different view. And then we'll have our last dinner tomorrow night. Howard would be *very* upset if he thought you were missing one minute of a good time!"

Olive straightened, looking back at Maggie. "You're right. I'm just being silly. Jack is angry, but there's nothing he can do about it. I *did* tell the captain about witnessing him putting the sandwich in Art's backpack, though."

Jean just groaned. "Jeez. Are you trying to audition for Court TV?" But then she reached over and patted Olive's shoulder. "I'm just teasing you. Everything will be fine."

Chapter 32

The food that night, while not as fancy as that of the gala, was delicious nonetheless. And while the women had enjoyed playing dress-up, they also enjoyed wearing simple pantsuits with lower heels.

The Countess and her companion actually joined them at the entrance that evening, so they had taken a table to accommodate five. Olive noticed that the Countess had motioned the young woman to sit to her left, away from the others, so it was difficult to direct questions her way.

"Oh, my!" they said in unison as they gazed at the food offerings. They all chose the shrimp cocktail, with Olive opting for the duck for her entrée while Maggie and Jean stayed true to their inner selves by ordering the prime rib.

Maggie discreetly brought their attention to the menu items chosen by the Countess. Jean smirked a little during dinner, watching the Countess eat quite a lot of food, obviously still maintaining an appetite despite her years.

The older woman's focus on her meal left little time for conversation, so the trio were content to discuss the day among themselves. All agreed that the dessert could wait until later with a nightcap in their room, although the Countess clearly had other ideas, adding a piece of cheesecake to her dinner order.

As they were being served their entrées, Maggie murmured, "Well, well, well. Looks like grief doesn't impede appetites," nodding in the direction of a table for two across the dining room. Jack and Bev had seated themselves while a server took their drink order. Jack wasn't even using his normal booming voice so the women couldn't eavesdrop on their conversation. Even the Countess looked over at Jack's table, grunting while she put a chunk of bread in her mouth.

Olive announced, "In keeping with Jean's instructions this afternoon, I refuse to pay any attention to them and will just enjoy my own evening."

Maggie, looking somewhat chastened, picked up her fork and knife, and sliced off a tender morsel of beef.

At that moment, a server appeared at their table with three glasses of red wine. "Compliments of the gentleman at that table, ladies."

Looking past the server they saw Jack give them a small salute, with Bev smiling at his side. The women nodded their thanks and went back to their meals.

As Jean's back was to Jack's table, she whispered, "That guy never ceases to amaze me. Next thing we know he'll want to join us for the quiz."

The Countess, obviously fortified by her meal, joined in the conversation. "I could not help but notice you this afternoon, Olive, coming up the hallway on our deck, with a steward and that American fellow. You all looked very worried."

Olive grimaced. "Yes, it was so sad. Jack, that fellow over there, told us he had misplaced his key and couldn't get his wife, Karen, to open the door, even though he called out to her, so we all went up to their suite and the steward let him in. Karen had told us that she was highly allergic to nuts of any kinds and it appears that she ate some Thai noodle dish with peanuts. She'd also told us about how terrifying it is to have an attack, because she felt like she was suffocating."

The Countess shook her head gravely. "But surely, being aware of her condition, she must have ordered a meal without nuts?"

"That is what Jack said, but I have to wonder about the whole scenario," Olive said.

"Hmm," was the Countess' only reply.

As Olive finished her meal, she took another look around the dining room and was surprised to see the Camera Man, wearing a sport jacket and tie, seated by himself at a table in the corner with a good view not only of the Countess and her companion, but of Jack and Bev, as well. This time he was *sans* camera.

When Bev got up, presumably to use the ladies' room, Olive noticed that the strange man waited a moment, and then also left the dining room.

Olive got Jean's attention and pointed unobtrusively toward him. In response to Jean's quizzical expression, Olive whispered, "Remember I told you about him talking with Bev earlier?"

Maggie just shrugged as she looked over at his departure.

Then Bev returned and sat down with Jack, not saying anything. Camera Man must have been done with his dinner, because he didn't come back. Olive then happened to glance down the table at the Countess's companion, who must have also noticed the departures, as her face betrayed a lot of emotion. The Countess continued on with her dessert, unfazed.

The women lingered over their coffee, while the Countess and her companion rose to return to their suite. Jean kept her eyes on her watch, so as not to miss the quiz, expecting the remaining Australians to partner with them again.

Walking into the pub, however, they were surprised by a voice behind them. "Ladies, if you don't mind, I'd like to join you." It was Jack! "Bev's gone up to her suite," he continued, "and the police are still in ours, so I might as well see what I know about trivia, you know, in Karen's honor."

Maggie recovered her composure first. "Sure," she stuttered. "We can use all the help we can get and hopefully there are some golf questions." Seeing the Australians move toward them she shook her head and they retreated to another table.

Seeing their disappointment, Olive resolved to explain to them later that they could team up the following night.

Jack, continuing his gallantry, insisted on buying each of them a glass of beer. Sitting across from Olive, he smiled at her, asking if she was enjoying the cruise.

"Yes. Very much so," she replied. "When my husband is feeling better, it would be wonderful to do it again, although, he did mention trying Cuba, if it's possible."

Jack smiled at her again. "I feel like kind of a heel. I didn't want to come on this cruise and made sure Karen knew it. I could have been a lot nicer about it."

Olive observed that Jack was something of a charmer when he modulated his voice and smiled. She could see how Karen would have fallen for him when they were young. But she wasn't going to be swayed by his abrupt change in attitude. She wasn't that gullible.

The quiz master announced the beginning of the contest, and the time was quite enjoyable, Jack being more broadly knowledgeable than the others would have guessed. When they came in second to the Australian team, Maggie raised her glass in congratulations. The question about the game of cricket was the deciding factor, and Jack spoke for all of them when he scoffed that cricket wasn't really a game, it was an excuse to drink tea.

The acoustic musician wasn't scheduled for another fifteen minutes, and the women hoped that Jack would leave, so Maggie asked, "Will the police let you back into your room tonight?"

"I sure hope so," Jack replied. "It's not that big a space and I'm not sure what they're looking for. I don't know what they're doing about our plates of food. I didn't even have time to try mine before I came down for the phone. You remember that, don't you? I ran into you while I was looking for it."

"Do you think they'll give you another room?" Jean asked innocently. "You can't stay up all night."

"Well, I'm not sure," Jack answered, with some hesitation. "I'm going up now to check. I'll have to make some kind of arrangement, I suppose." With that, he bade the women goodnight and walked toward the elevators.

Maggie burst out laughing. "Jean, you are a brat! Do you think he was going to tell you about the new sleeping arrangements?" She whirled around to Olive. "And Olive, don't you dare follow him!"

Jean grabbed for Olive as she stood up.

"It's alright. I'll be back," Olive insisted, disentangling herself from her twin sister. "I'm going to get my camera from the suite to take a photo of the musician and the jazz quintet, that's all."

Since hers was the next elevator after Jack's, Olive was able to peek out of it when it got to their floor— just in time to see Jack put his ear to the door of his own suite, and then proceed down to Bev's suite. After he went inside, Olive's curiosity got the better of her, and she quietly knocked on the door of Jack's suite. It was opened by the plainclothes detective.

"Oh, I'm sorry, officer," Olive said. "I was just looking for Jack Leonard."

"And who are you?" the detective asked.

"My name is Olive Reader. Jack was just playing the quiz with our team in the pub. Maybe he went next door?"

"Well, I'm a detective with the State police and we've secured his room until further notice." He paused. "Olive Reader. Aren't you the woman who spoke to the captain? Something about being suspicious regarding the death of Mrs. Leonard today and the death of another passenger back in Skagway? It sounds like you pointed the finger at Mr. Leonard, so I'm surprised you're friends with him."

"We were friends with his wife, having met them on this cruise," Olive clarified, "but for some reason he asked to join in the quiz tonight."

The detective looked at his notebook. "So, who's next door?"

"The widow of the man who died in Skagway."

The detective nodded slowly. "Oh. So did you meet her, too?"

"Just briefly."

"I know we'll want to talk to you, probably tomorrow sometime," he said. "I have my notes from speaking with the captain, but I'll want to clarify some points. We're just about finished with our search of this suite." He paused, and then smirked. "Don't go anywhere."

Olive laughed at his joke—she couldn't very well jump ship to avoid questioning—and made her way back down the hall to their suite to get her camera. She just wouldn't tell Jean or Maggie about her pit stop, that's all.

Chapter 33

As the Countess beckoned Annie toward the exit, she could not help but be struck by the beauty of the approaching sunset. The view from the table would have been wonderful, but she didn't wish to return to the dining room, having already made up her mind to return to the suite. But then she had a change of heart.

"Annie, go up to our suite and bring down sweaters for each of us. Hurry!" the Countess insisted. "I do not want to miss the sunset. I'll be over by the door on the promenade deck."

An looked around the Countess, startled to spy Li-Liang standing behind a pillar. "Yes, Madame, I will be right along."

She watched the Countess move toward the elevator to travel down to the promenade deck, allowing An to quickly walk over to Li-Liang, who apparently had already heard the exchange. He put his palms up to calm her, and then, unbeknownst to An, moved his left hand to his jacket pocket to caress its contents.

"Just do as your mistress says," he cautioned her, guiding An toward another elevator. "We will meet after she returns from her walk, so don't anger her by being late with her sweater."

The view from the promenade deck was spectacular. The sun had not yet fully set, so the coastline, although still somewhat distant, was a wonderful collage of green, with the blue of the water struggling to keep pace with the ever-growing hues of faint orange and deepening red provided by the descending dusk.

The Countess found that while the air was still fairly warm, she would need her sweater momentarily. Looking around impatiently, she spotted Annie racing toward her. "Annie, you stupid girl! Did you walk up and down the stairs?" she demanded.

Annie could only lower her eyes in what looked like fear. The Countess smirked triumphantly before taking back her room key and putting it into the pocket of her sweater.

Walking along the deck, with Annie trailing just behind her, the Countess slowed occasionally to fully appreciate the view. Her thoughts took her back to the coast of France and her anticipation in continuing her honeymoon there. With Heinz draping a soft wool shawl over her shoulders, both of them breathing in the warm, salty air and looking back at the white cliffs of Dover on the English side of the Channel, she remembered feeling so protected and loved, and hoping it would last a lifetime.

Well, it hadn't. Snapping out of her reverie, she growled at Annie. "Leave me! I will return to the suite in a little while."

An could only scuttle away, feeling for her own key, hoping to find Li-Liang and sit with him for a while.

After An had left him to retrieve her employer's sweater, Li-Liang had taken a seat to consider his options. He was tempted to follow An and remove the suitcase from the Countess' suite, but then he considered the dangers. What if the Countess decided to go up again and found it missing? But they still had one day aboard ship; then, in Vancouver, the porters would remove all the luggage before the passengers disembarked, and the Countess would not pay attention, to the number of suitcases, presumably, as An would have packed everything and set them outside the door for removal.

Li-Liang was a gambler, though. Perhaps for the time being, he could just follow the Countess and An in their walk, taking his time in making any decision. He paused for a moment and looked out at the water. The view *was* beautiful, no doubt. Such beauty was clearly wasted on the Countess; she would do better gazing at herself in the mirror while he strolled along the deck with An.

He rose from his seat to go find them.

Having dismissed Annie for the evening, the Countess continued her progress along the deck. She was startled to see so few other passengers on such a beautiful night. She decided to stroll around to the other side of the ship; perhaps there were more passengers interested in the lights of villages along the shoreline.

It didn't really matter, though, did it? People kept to themselves, so there wouldn't be much conversation at hand. As the sun was slowly setting, she still found it pleasant, so she decided to take one more turn around the ship.

Not too bad for an old lady, she thought, actually smiling to herself.

The captain had returned to his office after dinner, checking in with his junior officer on the bridge along the way. He loved his job—he'd loved it from the day he received his certification. Some of his colleagues enjoyed the social side, mingling with the passengers, while others much preferred to stay on the bridge, relating only to the crew and the sea. Luckily for him, he found something to like in each facet of his profession.

This week, however, was testing his patience. While the weather had been fantastic—no problems there— sickness and death were difficulties to deal with as part of his job.

Mr. Herrington's death in Skagway had not, at least technically, been a situation involving the ship. And the young Australian couple had obviously contracted typhoid somewhere in Africa—again, not a problem, technically, for the ship. But while Mr. Herrington's death was of no particular moment to other passengers, save for his wife and friends, the initial dire diagnosis, removal of the very ill couple by helicopter, and detour back to Skagway for blood testing of all passengers and crew, had provided him with excitement he could do without. He was proud of his staff, though. All of the passengers had responded positively to the testing, and the feedback he received told him he had done the right thing.

But now, there was the death of a passenger which *could* impact the cruise line. This was definitely a problem. He'd personally interviewed the kitchen staff and had been assured that the dishes were clearly marked. Before the steward removed the plates from the room service trays, the detective who had joined the ship in Skagway photographed all of the contents of the cabin table, for possible later use, while examining everything in the suite.

The captain sighed, and then chuckled to himself that maybe he was "getting too old for this ship."

The breeze was freshening out on the deck, but it was time to go in, the Countess decided as she rounded the last turn at the bow of the boat. It was now dark, and while the inner lights illuminated some of the deck, the bow area was surprisingly dark.

She stopped. Should she return to the more lighted

portion of the deck, or just forge on, having been in this area a couple of times already? She could see the outline of a couple of boxes up ahead, probably holding life jackets, if she recalled correctly.

The Countess felt a small tug on the back of her sweater, enough to put her a little off balance, and she stumbled forward. Trying to turn around, she realized that she was falling, and turned again to break her fall. Hitting her head on the deck, she grunted and tried to get up, but, sinking back again, very disoriented, she felt a short, sharp pain in her neck.

Chapter 34

"Our last day on the cruise!" Maggie exclaimed. "I want to do absolutely everything we can on this boat, and take lots more photos, too!"

Jean and Olive both laughed, giving her a thumbs up while moving back into the suite to refresh their coffee cups.

Olive was a little tired from a restless night. The events of the past couple of days had brought her some anxiety, just like she had felt during the Kinfolk matter, but she was determined not to give into it.

"Still no announcement from the medical team," she said to Jean and Maggie, "but maybe no news is good news? I *would* like to know if the young Australian couple is recovering, though. If I run into the detective, maybe he'll know."

The other women nodded as Olive shook herself to get out of her funk.

"I'm missing Howard and can't wait to get home, but it's exciting to know that we still have a full day ahead of us before we dock in Vancouver first thing tomorrow," Olive said, bringing the pot out to Maggie. After setting it down, she looked over the railing. "You know, we always look out at the shoreline, but it's interesting to actually look down the side of the ship toward the water," she said, gesturing to the other women to join her.

"Hmm, it's not as far down as I thought," mused Jean. "When we go out for our walk around the deck, let's see if we can get a better look."

They all peered over the edge together, taking in the view of the railings below and the water below that, rippling in the wash from the propellers. Looking out from the ship, they could see some recreational boaters.

Jean stepped inside to turn on the television to see where they were in relation to the coastal communities, and it showed a real-time map of their journey. "We're in Canadian waters, by the looks of it," she called out to the others, still on the veranda.

Jack glanced at his watch. The broads should be done with their breakfast by now, he thought, knocking on their door.

Maggie opened it, looking quizzical.

"Sorry, Maggie, I need to talk to you all for a couple of minutes," he said politely. "May I come in?"

Walking into the suite, Jack noticed all three of their room keys on the desk near the door. Maggie turned to speak to Jean, who tapped on the bathroom door to let Olive know they had company so she wouldn't just stride out from her shower. In that moment, Jack palmed one of the keys from the desk and slid it into his pocket.

He moved away from the desk toward the veranda, commenting on the day's bright sunshine. "Karen told me she was a little worried about the weather on the cruise, because apparently there's a higher risk of rain in August. She would have loved this day." His voice cracked a little and he wiped away a tear.

Olive came out of the bathroom in her robe. "Hello, Jack. How are you?" she said, trying not to sound too curt.

"I'm holding up, but it's Bev that I'm worried about," Jack said. "She just wants to stay in her room, and I don't think that's good for her. She'll be a real mess when Matt meets her at the airport. I was wondering if you could help her. Since we're not leaving the ship today, if we could all just coax her into joining us for a walk around the ship, and maybe dinner and that quiz thing tonight, it might cheer her up. She may even want to try the casino again, too. Since Karen died, it wouldn't look right for me to be coming and going from her suite too much, you know."

The women nodded. While they didn't particularly care for Bev, they were all caring people and agreed that they should reach out to comfort Bev in her time of need.

"Is she in her room now?" Jean asked.

"I assume so. The police let me back into our suite late last night, so I haven't been out until just now," Jack informed them. "We can go to Bev's suite, if you wish."

Olive told Jean and Maggie that they should go with Jack while she dressed. "We planned on taking our walk shortly, so why don't you see if Bev wants to join us?" she said.

After the group's departure, Olive dressed quickly. She was just about to join them in Bev's suite when she heard a knock at the door. Expecting it to be Jean and the others, she was startled to open the door to the Alaskan detective and a crew member.

"Come in, come in," she said, trying to regain her composure. "I forgot that you wanted to talk to me today."

"I'm not sure what to ask you, really, as it *does* appear that Mrs. Leonard inadvertently ingested some nuts and suffered anaphylactic shock," the detective said, stepping into the suite.

Olive shut the door behind him and the crew member and offered them coffee, but they both declined.

"Now, you mentioned your suspicions about Mr. Leonard regarding Mr. Harrington's death in Skagway," the detective said. "I think it would be helpful for me to hear your thoughts from the very beginning of your involvement with both couples. Perhaps there's something that will help us with our investigation."

"I'll do my best, detective," Olive said.

Just then, the door opened and the others trooped in, trailed by Jack and Bev. Olive studied Jack as he visibly blanched at the detective's presence.

The crew member nodded toward the party. "Despite the circumstances, I hope you can try to enjoy your last day aboard ship."

The detective said nothing, just gazed at Jack and Bev.

Olive cleared her throat. "The detective wants a few minutes with me, so why don't you all just start the walk and I'll join you shortly?"

Jack's head jerked toward her, his eyes narrowing and his jaw clenched. "Do you want me to stay too, in case there's something I can add?" he asked the detective.

"That won't be necessary, Mr. Leonard," the detective replied. "You gave a full statement last night."

Jack shrugged his shoulders and followed the women out of the room.

The detective turned to Olive, asking her again to try to remember everything she'd observed from first meeting the couples in Vancouver the day prior to departure.

Olive retraced the days, which now seemed so long ago, including spotting Jack putting a sandwich and juice in Art's backpack.

The detective nodded. "Mr. Herrington's pack was inventoried at the morgue. I'm having someone verify its contents as we speak. Please, go on."

Olive continued, bringing her narrative to the present, and then stopped in the middle of describing the scene in the Leonard's suite, when they discovered Karen's body. "I just thought of something," she said. "Did anyone from your team take photos?"

The detective nodded. "Of course."

"Jack and Karen were supposed to be sharing lunch. As I'm sure he told you, Karen ordered lunch and gave instructions about the allergy issue," Olive said, getting excited. "But what if *Jack* ordered lunch? And then he arranged the plates so that she would eat the wrong food? No, that wouldn't work, because it would be too easy to check. So we're back to square one. How about this—they get the same lunch, but there's only one without nuts, which Jack makes sure is on *his* side of the table, so Karen begins to eat, not realizing the food is contaminated."

The detective crossed his arms, just listening.

"Do you have a photo of the actual plates?" Olive asked. "When I saw the table, something struck me as odd, but I couldn't put my finger on it."

With a sigh, the detective reached into his briefcase and took out a digital camera. He showed Olive a picture of the Leonards' suite.

"Oh, yes—there it is!" Olive squealed, pointing at the image on the camera's screen. "See the plates? Jack's plate still has a cover on it, because he left the room to look for his cell phone near the pool— supposedly. And Karen was supposed to have begun her lunch without him. But see the spoons? His is not by his plate, unused. *Both* spoons are next to her plate and *both* appear to have been used." She looked up at the detective. "Do you think it's possible that Jack gave

Karen a little help in ingesting the nuts? According to what she told me about a prior incident, it wouldn't take much to cause a reaction.

The detective nodded slowly. "I see what you mean," he said. "I'll get the ship's doctor to help me examine Mrs. Leonard's body again, see if we can find any pressure marks."

"Pressure marks?" Olive echoed.

"If Jack was forcing her to swallow some of the food, as you said, there would probably be pressure marks on her head," the detective explained. "Now, I've told you enough. You should get going. Thank you for your help, Ms. Reader."

"You're right, I'd better join the walkers," Olive agreed. "Jack gave me a funny look when he saw us talking, but it probably doesn't mean anything. I still think he poisoned Art, but it sounds like you've hit a dead end there. Maybe he put the aconite, if that's what he used and if he has any left, in Bev's or Art's luggage after Art's death. Can you check there?"

"Not without Bev's consent," the detective replied. "Since Art died on land, their suite is not a crime scene, so we can't go through it without a search warrant. There has been no autopsy as of yet, though, what with all the crisis intervention required when the ship returned to Skagway, so I suppose I can suggest that Mrs. Herrington let us look through the suite in order to forestall the need to do an autopsy. If you don't think she had any involvement with all of this, she may allow us access. Anyway, if you see her, please tell her I'd like to talk to her. After I'm done with the doctor, I'll be in the chief steward's office."

Olive nodded, eager to help.

The detective began to open the door, but then he paused for a moment. "This has nothing to do with either the Leonards or the Herringtons, but are you familiar with a Countess Von Holbein, who was also a passenger on this cruise?" he asked.

"Was?" Olive looked puzzled.

"Yes. A crew member found her in the bow area this morning, out on the deck. The ship's doctor thinks she died late last night. She must have been walking by herself—although it was kind of late for an older lady to be out in the elements. I'm going to talk to her companion shortly." He opened the door and gave Olive a nod. "Have a good day, Ms. Reader."

The door closed behind him, but Olive was frozen. She was dumbfounded. The Countess was certainly in fine fettle at dinner. This cruise was turning into some kind of death watch!

Jack kept looking around the deck, pretending to enjoy the walk with Bev and the other women. Where the heck was Olive? How much could she have to talk about? He went back over his time aboard the ship, thinking of any lapses in his strategy. He'd been with Olive and her other Musketeers when Karen met her end, so they were his alibi.

Suddenly, Olive came into his view. He'd have to ask her what all the fuss was about—but carefully. She had more moxie than he'd first thought. He remembered that he had one of their suite keys; there was still time to take care of Olive, if need be. He'd just have to get her alone.

"So, aren't the police going to let you enjoy the rest of the cruise?" Jack asked Olive. He smiled broadly and shouted to the others to wait up.

Olive decided to play along. "I don't know why they're questioning me," she said innocently. "I guess because Karen died in your suite, they want to confirm every last detail. They went over our time by the pool, and your time there, too. I told them that you were looking for your cell phone, found it, and then went back up to have lunch with Karen. There really wasn't much else to say."

Jean approached Olive. "Take a look up the side of the ship, will you?" she said. "We just figured out that our suite is right there." She pointed up at a veranda about four decks above them. "Let's do another turn around the deck now that you've joined us. After that, I want to go up to the observation deck for a walk around there. I'm sure the view of the coast is pretty spectacular."

Bev and Jack trailed along behind them, and then followed the women into the elevator to the observation deck. Surprisingly, even they seemed awed by the view of the dense spruce forests framing the Passage itself.

Bev even added some commentary: "The steward told me that the Passage was formed millions of years ago by massive glaciers, so there are lots of fjords coming off of it. Apparently, it's fifteen kilometers wide, whatever that is in miles, and runs all the way from Puget Sound in Washington State to Skagway. The narrowest point is some hours south of Prince Rupert in British Columbia; it's called the Grenville Channel and it's only about fourteen hundred feet wide. I can see why they call it British Columbia—all these places have English names!"

Jean raised an eyebrow at Olive. Who knew Bev had such an interest in history?

Bev began to turn toward the elevators. "Well, this has been nice," she said. "Got me out of my room. I didn't feel like breakfast, so I should eat something now."

The group then heard an announcement over the loudspeaker. "Would passenger Beverly Herrington please come to the chief steward's office?"

Jack looked startled as Bev asked no one in particular, "I wonder what that's all about?"

"Do you want me to come with you?" Jack asked, putting his hand on her elbow. "I don't want anyone giving you any crap!"

Bev shook her head. "Actually, they have all been so kind to me. They did mention as we left Skagway that they'd pass on any information they get regarding whether there will be an autopsy for Art." She turned to leave. "I'll see you all later by the pool. I guess I can grab a burger there later."

Olive could see Jack's gaze following Bev as she got off the elevator to walk toward the chief steward's office. As the door closed, his head then swiveled toward Olive, giving her a start.

"Would you like to join us at the poolside to wait for Bev?" she stammered. "But I think we're going to our suite for a few minutes first."

"Sure," Jack said with a grin, but he didn't look happy. Olive fought not to shudder.

Back in the suite, Olive let out a long sigh. "I wonder if the detective plans to convince Bev to let him into her suite. I'd sure like to be a fly on that wall," she remarked.

Jean took Olive by the shoulders and gently shook her. "As I told you before, you've done your bit, so just relax and enjoy the rest of the day, for heaven's sake! I can hear Howard whispering to me over the miles, *Keep my Olive safe.* Got it?"

Remembering the detective, Olive started to share his information about the Countess' sudden death.

Just then, Maggie thought she heard something in the hallway, so she opened the door to see the detective pass by with Bev and a crew member at his side.

"Really, officer, I don't know what you hope to find in the suite, but feel free to look," Bev was saying, her voice carrying into the women's suite. "How long will you need? I haven't eaten today, so I want to go to the pool and have some lunch."

"I'm so sorry, Mrs. Herrington," the detective apologized, his voice also carrying. "Please, go about your business. I have a crew member here as a witness as I look around, so there's no need to trouble you."

Maggie called to Bev from the doorway of the suite. "We're headed to the pool as well, if you care to join us."

The women were delighted to spend the next couple of hours or so lolling by the pool. Bev appeared to enjoy herself as well, eating lunch and conversing with the group. She seemed to have become more affable, showing them a photo of her son and Art on a recent hike in New York, obviously very proud of Matt.

Jack happened along a short time after the women sat down, but spotting the loud fellow from the other day, joined him in the hot tub.

After a while, Jean stretched and stood, announcing that she was going up to their suite for a little nap before dinner. Glancing at Bev, Jean asked whether she wanted to join them for the last meal.

Bev nodded, appearing to appreciate the invitation. "Thanks, yes," she said. "I've eaten a lot of room service, it seems. That nap idea also sounds great. I'll head up, too."

Maggie and Olive nodded in agreement, so all of the women headed for the elevator. But about twenty feet from the elevator entrance, Bev veered off toward an Asian man, dressed in jeans and a golf shirt. Yes, it was the same man, Camera Man! Olive couldn't help but find it curious that they should be speaking so intently together.

Olive slowed her stride to get a better view, and saw Bev reach into her purse and give the man an envelope. Hearing Jean and Maggie call to her from the open elevator, Olive stepped up her pace to join them.

Pursing her lips at Jean's questioning glance, she said, "It's nothing—I should just mind my own business."

Jean looked over at Maggie and smirked. "Amen to that!"

Arriving at their suite, the women all lay down for a short while. Arising refreshed, Jean took out the remnants of the scotch and poured them each a small glass. They walked out onto the veranda to enjoy the view, and spotted a pod of whales.

Olive yelped, "I've got to get another couple of photos!" She rushed back into the suite to find her camera. "Did I take my camera to the pool?" she called back, searching frantically.

"It should be next to the keys on the desk," Maggie answered.

Olive found her camera there, but only saw Jean's key and her own, which she'd used to open the door. "I don't see your key here, Maggie," she said as she stepped back onto the veranda.

"That's strange," Maggie said, frowning. "All of our keys were on the desk this morning, but I didn't bother taking mine because we weren't leaving the ship today. Hmm . . . When we go down to dinner, I'll check with the steward to see if someone turned it in."

Chapter 35

Li-Liang patted An on the shoulder, telling her gently to stop crying.

She had practically run into his arms last night, so needy and trusting. Freed of her mistress for the rest of the evening she had been almost babbling with excitement. It had not been difficult to convince her that a real drink, not just a beer, would settle her nerves. He'd gone to the bartender and ordered a tropical drink, paper umbrella and all, laced with a lot of rum.

An was clearly not a drinker. Li-Liang had only briefly left her at the table, and upon his return, found her asking for another drink. Once she'd consumed most of the second drink, he was able to guide her back to his cabin. He left her unconscious in his bed while he ordered a beer from room service.

Now An was distraught, finding herself in his bed and fighting a horrible hangover. She wasn't even sure what to call it, the effects of alcohol being so new to her.

"My mistress will fire me!" she cried. "She will expect me to be in our suite!"

Li-Liang again tried to calm her. "You drank a lot last night, so it was all I could do to get you into my cabin," he said. "Would you want the old lady to find you drunk and unconscious?" He'd ordered toast and coffee for the both of them, hoping that it would revive An's spirits.

There was a knock at the door. Li-Liang answered it tentatively, trying to shield An from any visitors.

Seeing it was a steward and another man in a suit, he inquired, "What can I do for you?"

An drew up the covers around her, cringing.

"We are trying to locate this woman," said the man in the suit, showing Li-Liang a photo of An. He also flashed a detective's badge. "The steward thought he recognized her during room service earlier this morning."

Li-Liang opened the door to them and they entered.

"I'm sorry to bother you, Miss," the detective said to An, "but are you traveling with Countess Von Holbein?"

An stared at him. "Yes, I work for her."

"Then I regret to tell you that she died sometime last night while walking on the promenade deck."

An gasped. "But that can't be! After dinner she told me to bring her a sweater and to leave her to walk alone." Turning to Li-Liang she motioned and added, "Since I had the rest of the evening off, I met with Li-Liang and had a drink. Then we came to his room."

The detective again nodded. Yeah, right. Just one drink.

The steward asked if he could be excused, so the detective stepped out as well, leaving An to rise and wobble to the bathroom. Knowing they would both be questioned further, she decided to shower, hoping to remember more from the night before.

Chapter 36

"Little sister, you look positively stunning!" Jean exclaimed when Olive came out of the bathroom. "The blouse that Howard picked out looks so great on you!" She patted Olive's shoulder and Maggie wolf-whistled.

"You'll give me a big head!" Olive responded, blushing. But she could only agree that Howard had made the right choice. The long sleeved white blouse had a scoop neck and silver threads running through the material. Her grey hair, now running closer to white, also went well with the top. Howard had gone shopping while she was at the passport office and had surprised her with it before she left for the trip.

Hearing a knock at the door, Maggie opened it to find the detective waiting expectantly. "We've got to stop meeting like this!" she said, receiving a rather blank look. "Oh, well, I guess you had to be there," she muttered, and invited the detective into the suite.

"Just thought I'd stop by with an update," he said.

"Oh, that's wonderful!" Olive exclaimed. "The blood tests are negative and the young couple is going to recover?" she asked hopefully.

The detective paused. "Yes. I probably shouldn't say anything, because the captain is going to make an announcement very shortly, but apparently they were suffering from typhoid. They've both responded well to heavy-duty antibiotics, so they're out of the woods. No one else has been infected, so the captain will report on both matters, as he wants everyone to relax and enjoy their last night aboard the cruise.

"But that's not why I'm here," he continued. He held out his hand toward Olive, revealing a small vial only partially filled with some liquid. "We found this in Mr. Herrington's luggage and questioned Mrs. Herrington. We don't know what it is yet, and she seemed dumbfounded about its presence there, so we'll have to wait until we arrive in Vancouver to have it tested."

"I suppose it wouldn't do any good to question Jack Leonard about it, just to get his reaction?" Olive queried. She took the vial and turned it in her hand, but there were no markings on it indicating either the contents or the vendor. "He'd probably deny any knowledge of it."

"Are you dining with either Mrs. Herrington or Mr. Leonard this evening?" the detective asked. "I'm on my way back to the chief steward's office right now, but I just want to get a sense of your plans for tonight in case I have to catch up with you."

"They may ask to join us, and if so, we can't really refuse," Maggie responded. "The Countess has been dining with us, but . . ." She trailed off, and then shook herself. "After dinner, we normally go to the pub quiz and stay for the music, and after that, we listen to jazz in the lounge until later in the evening. When you return to the chief steward's office, could you ask whether anyone has turned in my suite key? I can't seem to find it."

The detective sighed. "Since it's on my way, yes. But you should really ask a steward about it."

"I don't remember taking it anywhere," Maggie murmured, more to herself than to anyone in the room. "Since we weren't leaving the ship today, I had no particular reason to bring it, as Olive had hers. It was on the desk this morning with the other keys, before you arrived. Jack had just stopped by." She gasped. "Wait! That's right! Jack came in here while Olive was showering, asking us to invite Bev along on our walk. He would have passed by the desk. But why would he want our key?"

A silence hung in the room.

"I'll check with the steward in any event," the detective said. "You all enjoy your evening and I'll touch base with you later if I need to."

After the detective closed the door behind him, the women all exchanged puzzled looks.

Olive spoke for all of them. "This just gets curiouser and curiouser. Well, I'm not going to let it bother me. We'll be in public places all evening, so I intend to eat, drink, and be merry!"

Maggie and Jean rallied as well. "Here, here!" they chorused.

The dining room was as beautiful as ever. "The ship must have a cold storage room for flowers, because every evening the room has a different look," Olive mused as she and the others waited to be seated. They chose a smaller table this evening, not really wanting to talk to Jack; they were sure that he would escort Bev to dinner, in any event.

As they were perusing the menu, Maggie murmured, "Incoming—Tweedle Dee and Tweedle Dum."

Jean and Olive looked up to see Jack and Bev being seated at a table for two. They noticed that Jack kept looking over at their table, so Jean put on a big smile and waved, hoping he would concentrate his attentions on Bev. It seemed to work.

The meal, as usual, offered so many wonderful choices. Maggie could only sigh. "I will never be able to read the Flushing Meadows menu board again without weeping just a little. All of these choices and such great flavors!" she exclaimed. "At least Olive and Howard have their grill and their garden—I'm so jealous! We're stuck with whatever the chef chooses for that day."

Jean snorted. "Oh, come on! Like you or I ever cooked much when we had our own homes. And a garden, for heaven's sake—so funny! But I am going to miss this cruise food, that's for sure."

Olive grinned. "I know you two will probably opt for the shrimp cocktail and the roast beef, which are tempting, but I'm going to see if it's alright to order the soup, one of the salads and one of *each* of the starters, instead of a meal. How can I go wrong?"

"You scamp!" Jean giggled.

With the dusk of the evening falling outside, the dining room raised its lights just a little, and the women enjoyed strains of a piano playing in the background. Jack again sent over three glasses of wine, to which the women smiled their appreciation. They would wait to find out whether he and Bev wanted to join them in the quiz.

The server having assured her that ordering multiple starters in lieu of dinner was not that uncommon, Olive felt pure bliss as each item was brought in turn. Meanwhile, Jean and Maggie happily sawed away at huge portions of beef.

"Dessert or no dessert, that is the question," Olive sighed as she finished the last of her food.

"Let's have coffee here and then make a room service request for slices of cheesecake," Jean suggested. "It's all too good to pass up."

Over coffee, Olive's thoughts drifted back to the Countess; surprisingly, she found herself missing the old woman, in a way. While she could be gruff, and her behavior with her employee was certainly disturbing, the Countess was an interesting woman, and appeared to be mellowing in the course of time.

Looking across the room, Olive noticed the Camera Man, *sans* camera, and the Countess' companion sitting across from each other at a corner table, somewhat in the shadows.

Olive motioned discreetly to Jean, pointing out the two diners.

"The couple appear to be arguing about something," Jean observed. "I wonder what the young woman will do now that her employer has died. Hopefully the Countess made some provision for her in a will. Who knows—maybe the young couple will just live happily ever after?"

Looking at her watch, Maggie glanced at the others and motioned toward the door. "We have to pass Jack's table on the way out, so to be sociable, let's tell them we're going to take part in the quiz. We can invite the Australian pair to join us, and if Jack and Bev come along, they can just be part of the team." Both Bev and Jack told them they'd stop by, but might opt for a last evening of gambling.

Olive wondered whether Bev had told Jack about the vial found in Art's luggage. *She has to be curious,* Olive thought, sure that Jack was behind Art's death. Obviously Jack couldn't explain the vial's presence to her. Would it occur to Bev that Jack might be responsible? Probably, not knowing the vial's contents, she might just think it was something Art had packed for his hikes.

But Olive couldn't shake her nagging uneasiness about Bev's meetings with the Camera Man, either. It was all a little strange. Bev had laughed heartily at Jack's racist jokes about "Orientals" earlier, so she couldn't imagine her having Asian friends, but according to Art, she did have some Asian clients.

Just let it go, Olive chided herself.

Walking into the pub area, the women heard a whoop from one of the tables. Sure enough, it was the two Australians waving them over.

"Hey, partners!" Maggie called out in response. "Let's move to that larger table over there; the two people who joined us last night may stop by."

The Aussies had obviously been imbibing—a lot— ostensibly to celebrate Alice and Arnie's medical status, knowing that though the couple was not entirely out of the woods, their recovery was proceeding well. And the fact that they themselves had not been infected made even more reason to celebrate, although Olive had to chuckle that tomorrow, their quiz teammates might truly feel under the weather.

As the announcer began asking questions, Olive spotted Bev leading Jack toward them. "We won't stay long," Bev said as they sat down at the table, "but hopefully there's a golf question tonight."

While Bev appeared to enjoy being part of the team, Jack was distracted, looking over at the glass windows into the casino situated some feet away. His smile was more of a grimace when Olive caught him looking toward her. No doubt the detective's presence on the ship was weighing heavily on him—or perhaps that was just her imagination.

She gave herself a small shake. Get over yourself, for heaven's sake!

As the quiz was ending, it was clear that Jack had had enough. He touched Bev on the shoulder and pointed toward the casino. "We may see you later to hear some jazz, but it'll depend on how much money I'm winning," he said, smiling at the group. He and Bev got up to leave.

The women sat back and watched the acoustic performer until they heard the tinkling of the piano from the jazz lounge. After finding a seat in that venue, they ordered cocktails, laughing that they were going to go on the wagon when they returned home.

Just after their cocktails had been served, they looked up to see the detective entering the room. He nodded to the trio, and the server took his order as he crossed the dance floor to join the women.

"Any news?" Olive asked when he sat down with them.

"Well, the ship's doctor told me he's always been interested in Chinese medicine, so he's done some research," the detective said. "He says that the dark blue, purplish substance in the vial is consistent with aconite. He took a small taste of it and confirmed it also has the somewhat bitter taste and tingling effect on the tongue that's supposed to accompany ingestion. So if it's poison, Mr. Herrington wouldn't have eaten it on purpose. He agreed that the bitterness could probably be masked by something spicy—hot mustard or the like."

He paused and grimaced. "But here's the problem. The morgue faxed the inventory of the backpack. It *did* contain a sandwich and juice, but *neither* were opened. I've asked them to test Mr. Herrington's blood and the lunch for aconite as a priority before the ship returns to Vancouver, so I should have the results shortly. That's all we have for now, so don't let me spoil the music for you. Cheers!"

With that, they all sat back and drank their cocktails, the detective included. Olive's mind was racing. She'd wait on the test results before telling the detective about Camera Man.

Jack happened to look through the doorway of the casino and spotted the red of Jean's trousers. Then he saw the foot of a man next to her. Peering around a column near the door, he blanched to see the detective sitting next to the women. What was that all about?

"Jack, are you not wanting to gamble?" Bev tugged at his sleeve.

You have no idea, he thought darkly.

Chapter 37

During dinner, Li-Liang and An were deep in conversation, barely noticing the dishes being served. Although the effects of her hangover had abated somewhat, An's grief about the Countess' mysterious death made her want to crawl under the covers somewhere, not sit in all of this splendor. Li-Liang was very attentive, insisting that she "dress up a little" for the dining room, and had ordered her a rye whisky and ginger ale, something he referred to as the "hair of the dog." She was surprised to find that it did settle her stomach—probably the ginger ale.

That morning, after the detective had left Li-Liang's cabin, she had taken a shower. Walking out of the bathroom, she'd heard the door unlock and witnessed Li-Liang carrying in the Countess' suitcase and putting it into the closet next to the door.

Her mind still being a little fuzzy, she'd wondered how he had gotten into the Countess' suite, but in the hurry of dressing to return to the suite herself, she'd only stepped back into the bathroom and did not give it further thought. Fully dressed, she had picked up her sweater and felt the key in its pocket. "Oh, there you are," she'd murmured.

An had wanted Li-Liang to accompany her to the suite, old superstitions making her fearful of meeting the Countess' ghost. He'd scoffed, telling her, "There are no such things as ghosts, and we don't want anyone assuming that we had something to do with her death." Reluctantly, she had left quietly, but before taking the elevator, she'd decided to check out the promenade deck, still not believing that her mistress had died there the night before.

Walking along the deck, she had struggled with her emotions. Why did she feel so sad? The Countess had never shown her any respect, let alone friendship—or even love, given that An had been in her household since childhood. But since that life was all she knew, she was beginning to miss it.

On a more practical level, what would she do when the ship reached Vancouver? Old Jiaying would have no idea of the Countess' death. She must tell her gently, though, as the other servant had no relatives in Canada either, so she was in the same boat, so to speak, as An was now.

An assumed that the grandnephew the Countess had met in Skagway was her only heir. Perhaps he would come to live in the house and keep both An and the cook employed to care for the place? Only time would tell.

An had been surprised that she had walked so far along the promenade deck; she was almost at the bow. Looking around, she'd half expected to see yellow tape, like in the movies, but then she shook herself.

This is *not* the movies, she'd thought. Will they want me to identify her, or are the photo identification cards sufficient? She assumed that the Countess had been carrying hers at the time of her death.

Li-Liang was watching An stare at nothing over the dinner table. He quietly munched on his salad, actually a little hungry.

He was willing to give the girl some space. It was all quite a shock, for sure. But they had to do some planning, so he called her name gently and took her hand, trying to get her attention.

Startled, An looked at him, squeezing his hand in response. "I went to the promenade deck after I left you this morning, to see where the Countess died," she admitted. "On the way back to the elevator, I thought I saw you talking to that woman whose husband died earlier. The women the Countess and I dined with told her all about the fellow hiking and having some kind of seizure."

Li-Liang continued to hold her hand, shaking his head. "You must have still been ill from the liquor," he said. "I don't know the woman you are talking about."

An nodded slowly. "I guess so, but didn't you also meet with her during dinner recently?" she asked. "I saw you leave the restaurant right after she did, and you never came back."

Li-Liang reddened somewhat and snorted derisively. "Are you becoming a spy or something? Haven't I been helping you find a future for yourself? I refuse to be questioned like this!"

Hearing him raise his voice, An rushed to apologize, not wanting to anger him. She might require his protection in the future, and she not only found him attractive, but much more sophisticated than she. Regardless, she did have one more question which she felt she must ask. "Why did you remove the suitcase of gowns from our suite to your cabin? The nephew will no doubt ask about it, and I don't want to be accused of stealing. I just hope that he will be grateful to me for keeping it safe and will reward me."

This was a turn of events that Li-Liang had not anticipated. "You have no guarantee that he will be generous," Li-Liang countered. "Has the Countess ever been generous? Is luggage not lost all the time? Is it possible that some other passenger may have taken the suitcase in error? Think of your future!" He then took An's hand again, this time very tenderly, speaking softly. "Think of *our* future . . ."

"But why can't I just keep it in our suite?" An asked, puzzled.

"You are a wonderful, silly girl." Li-Liang forced a grin, trying to appear relaxed. "I was worried that the authorities might search your suite sometime today to catalogue the Countess' belongings. She didn't die in the suite and there is no suggestion of foul play, so they probably won't, but this is just a precaution. You and I can leave the ship separately and then meet up later. I will give you my address and some cab fare. Alright, my dear?"

An nodded in agreement, albeit reluctantly, and began to pick at her dinner.

Chapter 38

Maggie looked over at the detective in between numbers by the jazz group. "Did you happen to mention my suite key to the chief steward?" she asked. "I suppose since we're leaving the ship early tomorrow morning it doesn't really matter, but I am kind of curious."

"No one has turned it in, apparently," the detective said.

Olive used the quiet of the musicians to interject, chuckling: "Remember that television show, *The Love Boat*? All fun and games? I can't help thinking about our poor captain. First Art dies on a hike. Then Karen dies, supposedly of an allergic reaction. Then the elderly Countess keels over! Wow!"

They all shook their heads, with the detective adding, "Frankly, even the death of the Countess is troubling me. Anyone can fall down and hit their head, but that didn't kill her. The steward who found her didn't touch her until we were able to see the situation for ourselves. She appeared to have been writhing— probably in a lot of pain—before she actually died. Yet although the bruise was on the front of her head, she was in a contorted position, more on her side, when we found her. With your questions about Art Herrington's death and the description the hikers gave about his body's condition when they found *him*, there are some similarities. But that has to be a coincidence."

The jazz group launched into a new number, so the detective and the women fell silent again. Although the detective was reasonably attentive to the women, Olive couldn't help but notice him glance around the room and the common area outside the venue every once in a while.

Just then, a young crew member walked up to their table. "Sir, the Chief asked me to give you this fax. I'll wait while you read it, in case you want me to bring any message back to him."

The women looked on expectantly while the detective reviewed the fax, wanting him to share the contents with them.

Exhaling dramatically, the detective looked at Olive. "Well, Olive, your research was right on the money. The substance is aconite and it showed up in Mr. Herrington's blood, but since the sandwich and juice were unopened, we can't lay that at Mr. Leonard's door. But here's the other thing: the coroner found a small puncture in the back of Mr. Herrington's neck, which is a strange place for one, even if he was some kind of user. We know he probably wasn't, because there were no traces of any kind of narcotic substance in his system."

"What if someone followed him on the trail and knocked him down before injecting him?" Olive interjected. "Art isn't alive to name anyone as an assailant."

"Well, we now know it wasn't Jack Leonard," the detective countered. "He was golfing during that time, and not only can Mrs. Herrington give him an alibi, I'm sure the golf course pro shop can verify the time the golfers arrived and left the course."

Olive shrugged. "I haven't shared this until now, but I've seen Bev Herrington talking with an Asian man at least two times. At their last meeting, they both appeared to be agitated, with Bev taking an envelope out of her purse and giving it to the fellow before he walked off."

Maggie spoke up with another question. "Isn't he also the one who's spending time with the Countess' companion? You mentioned that earlier when we saw them together."

"So you would recognize a photo of him?" the detective asked. "She was in his cabin this morning when we went looking for her." The detective turned toward the crew member and began giving instructions.

Olive tapped the detective on the shoulder. "If he can bring not only the passenger photos, but a list of people who disembarked on shore excursions—or just for some other purpose when we docked in Skagway— we can see if the man was among them," she suggested. "Also, we should know when the passengers returned to the ship. I don't want to point a finger at someone for Art's death who just might be innocent, like I did with Jack."

The detective nodded toward the crew member. "Got that? And if I'm not here when you return, just give the stuff to these women so they can start going over the information."

The musicians began playing a more spirited number, inviting listeners to dance.

Olive grinned at the others. "While we're waiting for the information from the chief steward, I'm going to run to our suite to get my camera. These dancers should be captured live to show to Howard. Maybe it will inspire him to take me dancing sometime."

Before anyone could respond, she jumped out of her seat and hurried to the elevators.

The detective gazed at her departure, his brow furrowing. "I don't have a good feeling about this," he said, turning toward Maggie and Jean.

Then Jean gasped. "I think I just saw Jack walking toward the elevators! I thought he was in the casino."

The detective leapt up and strode quickly toward the casino. Looking inside, he spied Bev at one of the slot machines. She began to smile at his approach, but then stopped when he asked if Jack was there with her.

"He was, but he stepped out for a moment to use the bathroom," she said. "He said he was coming right back to do some more gambling. Is anything wrong?"

Bev didn't receive an answer, as the detective had already left the casino. He quickly walked toward the elevators. A sign in front of one of them said "Out of Order," so he had to wait for the next one. Jean and Maggie rushed up behind him.

Chapter 39

Olive let herself into her suite and decided to use the bathroom before returning to the jazz lounge. But stepping back into the sitting room, she gasped at seeing Jack standing there, a snide grin on his face.

"Well, well, well. If it isn't Miss Marple," Jack said menacingly. "Just full of information about Karen and what plates were where—my favorite busybody."

Olive tried to move toward the door. "How did you get in here?"

"You ladies are rather careless with your keys, you know. All set out on the desk waiting for me to borrow one." He moved toward her. "Now, we don't have much time."

As he was much bigger and stronger, Jack was able to lift Olive and drag her from the sitting room onto the veranda. In shock, Olive tried to call out, but could only manage a grunt as he banged her against the railing.

He began to lift her onto the cold metal, but she kept struggling. Finally, he was able to position her on the top of the railing. At that point, she could look out into the darkness below, hearing the lapping of the waves. As he started to push her, she finally managed a scream, and then another one, hoping that people in adjacent verandas would hear her cries for help.

In the midst of her fog of fear, it occurred to her that *Jack* had the adjacent veranda, and probably most of the folks would either be in the dining room or at other venues on the ship, anyway. She fought as hard as she could to hold onto Jack's coat, but could feel him pushing her off.

As Olive felt herself falling feet first from the railing, she tried to stay calm and remember her swimming and diving training from childhood. Her mother had insisted on it, and when her own son was young, Olive had taken him to the pool to do the same. As she went downward she tried to orient herself, feeling the cool air rushing at her and hearing the waves draw closer.

At the elevators, Maggie, Jean, and the detective tried to quell their anxiety during the interminable wait. The detective pulled out his cell phone to call the chief steward to see if there were personnel on Olive's deck who could go to the suite immediately. The elevator finally arrived, but with other passengers going from one venue to another, it stopped on practically every floor.

Jean began to sniffle. "If that schmuck harms one hair on her head, I'll kill him!" she growled, much to the surprise of the other occupants of the elevator.

After Jack saw Olive fall from the railing, he rushed out of the suite, careful to wipe off the key and leave it next to the lamp on the desk. Then he opened his own suite and slipped inside, all before the elevator doors opened down the hall.

As Olive neared the water, she was able to yell out another cry for help before she submerged. She bent double, holding her ankles in a crash position, hoping that she wouldn't break her neck. She took what might be her last breath just before she entered the water.

A couple of people on the promenade deck yelled in response to her scream, horrified by the sight of a fellow passenger falling into the water. A woman yelled for a steward, while her male companion ran down the deck, trying to keep his eyes on the victim, shouting, "Man overboard!" all the while. Luckily, the clear, full moon and Olive's white-and-silver blouse enabled him to keep track of her. He grabbed a life preserver and threw it as far as he could in her direction.

Olive had initially disappeared into the water before bobbing up, suddenly very cold, but still able to move her legs and arms. She tried to steady herself, remembering not to flail and to try to breathe easily, even though the wash from the ship made it difficult. *There was no point in calling out*, she thought, but she did shout once, just in case.

She let herself float and watched in disbelief as a life preserver appeared near her. She swam toward it, sobbing in gratitude.

Jean used her key to burst into their suite. She looked into the bathroom on the way through the open door to the veranda, where she turned to the detective. "I know we shut the veranda door before we left, so as not to cool down the suite too much during the evening!" she blubbered.

The detective looked over the edge of the railing, hearing some commotion below. Then he strode out toward Jack's suite, knocking heavily on his door. It took a moment or so for the door to open and the detective continued in, with Maggie and Jean directly behind him.

"What have you done with my sister?" Jean demanded, her voice cracking. She threw herself toward Jack.

He put up his hands to protect himself. "I don't know what you're talking about!" he retorted. "I left Bev in the casino for a couple of minutes to use the bathroom up here, and now I'm going back to join her. We planned to catch up to you later in the lounge. What are you doing in my suite?"

"We can't find Olive!" Maggie moaned.

"Well, I'm sorry," Jack said, not sounding sorry at all. "Where did she go? I thought she was with you in the lounge. Now, if you'll excuse me, I'm going back to the casino."

Maggie and Jean looked helplessly at the detective as Jack closed the door behind him. The detective called the chief steward's office to ask that a crew member be assigned to keep track of Jack, although he muttered to the women that Jack really couldn't go anywhere.

While waiting for the steward to answer the phone they heard the ship's horn sound loudly and heard running in the hallway. The ship's speed noticeably slowed. A steward almost bumped into them as he rushed into the suite and out to the veranda to look over the railing. He yelled at the women, "Man overboard!"

The detective and the women crowded next to him, while he breathlessly brought them up to date. "A woman fell from this deck, but she yelled and some people on the promenade deck spotted her. Someone threw out a life preserver, but they're not sure if she got it. It's August, so the water isn't freezing, but hypothermia is a killer!"

Jean started running toward the elevator, yelling at the steward, "Take us to the deck closest to the water! Has anyone put out a life boat or anything?"

Olive had been able to grab onto the life preserver, so she assumed someone on board must have seen her. But the ship kept moving away from her, and while she could see the shore because of the narrowed point in the channel, she knew she could not even try to reach it.

She was beginning to feel very cold and clammy. "No, no. I can't die like this," she whimpered. "Oh, Howard. I miss you so much!"

She tried to calm herself, understanding that she had to preserve her body warmth and just tuck herself into the preserver as much as possible.

Jack put his arms around Bev's shoulders when he came up behind her in the casino.

She leaned back against him. "Well, you took a while," she remarked. "You missed seeing me hit the jackpot."

"No I didn't," he laughed.

Bev turned around, looking quizzical.

"Let's go to the jazz lounge and have a drink," Jack said. "We can come back later."

When the detective, Jean, and Maggie arrived on the lower deck, crew members were already dispatching a life boat and attaching a small outboard motor to it. With the ship's engines slowing, they were able to drop the boat into the water fairly quickly. Two of the crew jumped in, one carrying blankets. The boat had a large lamp in the bow.

Maggie and Jean could only wait with the others, anxiously hoping that Olive was still alive. The ship's horn had stopped blowing, so at least it was quieter.

The detective looked over at Jean and Maggie and grabbed two blankets from another pile. "Wrap these around you," he instructed. "We don't want to rescue your sister only to have you both get pneumonia, for heaven's sake."

Seeing his rueful smile, they both managed thankful grins, tears streaming down their cheeks.

Jack and Bev clinked glasses as he proposed a toast. "To our future happiness! We'll see each other, but keep it discreet, the way we've been doing—at least until the kids get used to the idea of Art and Karen being gone. After that, we can go out in public, too. I'm sure that Jack Jr. will take it pretty hard to begin with, but he'll get used to it. And he's dating some girl he seems to like, so he'll get on with his own life and we can get on with ours."

The band began playing *Stardust,* and Jack asked Bev to dance.

"Should we?" she asked.

Jack chuckled. "It's actually the only thing I enjoyed doing with Karen, but I know I'll like this more."

He glided her around the floor, stroking her hair.

Just then, he noticed an Asian fellow, first standing by the corner of the lounge with a younger Asian woman, and then later when both of them had taken a seat. The whole time, the man's eyes were on Bev.

"That guy is staring at you, babe. Do you want me to ask him what his problem is?" Jack asked.

Bev just shook her head and turned back toward their table to take a sip of her cocktail.

Olive felt chilled to the bone. Luckily, she hadn't swallowed a lot of sea water, and she continued to grasp the life preserver, but she was painfully aware that soon, her fingers would be so cold that she might lose her grip.

The ship seemed so distant now. How long could she stay alive?

Wait a minute—was she hallucinating? In the distance Olive thought she saw a light of some sort. Weren't you supposed to see a bright light in a tunnel or something when you died? But it was coming closer. She began to hear voices, as well. She decided to use the last of her strength to call out. It was quiet out here, so maybe her voice would carry? "Help me!" she croaked out, waiting for a reply.

She could only watch as the light began to draw ever nearer. But then, it started to veer toward shore. She yelled again, and this time the light seemed to hesitate and turn toward her. Soon the light was almost too bright, and she heard someone call out, "There's something over there!"

In a couple of moments, strong hands were lifting her into the boat. She was helpless from the cold—she had almost passed out, in fact. But soon they had her settled in the boat and wrapped in thick blankets. Teeth chattering, she could only muster a "T-t-t-thank you."

Soon the cruise ship itself came into view. It was then that Olive began to weep, thankful that she would be reunited with everyone she loved. She also found herself *very* angry, which helped warm her all the more.

Stretching out her body, she lifted her arms and legs, confirming that she had no broken bones—although she knew there would be bruises. Coming alongside the ship, the life boat was pulled up beside the deck, where crew members gently lifted her toward a stretcher. She sat on it initially, as Maggie and Jean ran over, their tears joining the salt water in her hair. She grabbed hold of them and stood up, even though they begged her to lie down until she could be examined thoroughly.

Surprising even herself, she shouted and stripped off the blankets. "No way! I'm fine," she growled. "We are going back to the lounge to finish that cocktail! In fact, I'm going to order a double scotch in celebration, and detective, you're invited to join me. I hope we run into Jack Leonard on the way, because I have some news for him."

The detective stared at Olive in disbelief. "Forgive me for saying this, but you are one tough lady!" he chuckled. "When we saw Mr. Leonard walking after you, we tried to follow him, but with the elevator causing trouble, your suite was empty by the time we reached it. When we tried Mr. Leonard's suite, he said he had been in his bathroom."

"Well, he paid a visit to our suite first," Olive said sourly. "He must have used Maggie's key, because he followed me in. Before he pitched me off the railing on the veranda, he ranted at me for talking with you about my suspicions. I guess I'm a loose end he had to tie up. You know, I wouldn't be surprised if Jack and Bev are sharing a beverage in the lounge as we speak. He'll be one shocked 'so and so' when I walk into the room."

The detective, Maggie, and Jean all spoke together: "And we wouldn't miss it for the world!"

Jack and Bev decided to stay in the lounge for another cocktail. The ship had slowed somewhat, but now appeared be gaining speed again. The jazz group had begun playing the ballad *I'll Be Seeing You,* so the couple decided to enjoy another dance.

Jack was slowly whirling Bev around the floor when he heard a female voice behind him: "Hello, Jack. You and I did some dancing earlier this evening, didn't we?"

Jack let go of Bev, and spotting Olive behind him, headed for the door.

The detective and a crew member intervened. "Take this man into custody," the detective ordered.

"What are you doing?" Bev asked anxiously, now alone on the dance floor. "Jack? What is this all about?"

Jean broke in. "Your boyfriend here just tried to kill my sister!" she barked. "And he killed his wife, too! Do you think he's so special now? But then, you can always visit him in prison!"

Bev looked flabbergasted. "This can't be! Karen died of her allergies." She turned to Jack. "Jack! Tell me this is all a lie!"

The Camera Man had begun to rise from his seat, sidling toward the common area, but Olive spotted him. Pointing at him, she quickly yelled, "Stop that man!"

The detective, realizing that Olive was pointing at the Asian fellow, strode over and grabbed him by the arm before he could move any further.

"Is this the man you recognized earlier?" he asked.

Olive nodded as a young crew member handed her some sheets of paper. She rapidly sifted through them. "Here is the list of people who left the ship for the day in Skagway." She began going back and forth between the photocopied ID cards until she stopped. "Aha! So our friend, here—Mr. Feng, is it? Well, sir, it looks like you left the ship in Skagway shortly after Arthur Herrington departed for his hike. And, yes, you already knew what he looked like, didn't you, because you had plenty of time to observe him on the trolley tour in Vancouver," Olive said triumphantly. "Why didn't you just join us for a beer that day at the pub on Granville Island? It would have been so much easier than skulking around. What is your game, mister?"

From behind them they heard a wail, a plaintive woman's voice keening, "What is going on?" The Countess' young companion came up to them.

Li-Liang Feng dropped his head for a moment. Then he looked directly at Olive, not saying a word—just glaring at her.

She continued. "The State police know all about the aconite, Mr. Feng. And I'm sure the police are going to speak to all the hikers who were on the trail. One of them is sure to have seen you. You should know that Bev was foolish enough to keep the rest of the poison in

Art's luggage, maybe in case you failed the first time. Maybe even to use it on you!"

At that, the man quickly looked over at Bev, and though she motioned for him to be quiet, Olive had clearly touched a nerve.

The Camera Man cried out, "It was her doing! I was in debt to a syndicate of gamblers in Vancouver. That lady came here from New York, and I was told to work with her to pay off my debt, or suffer the consequences. She is not going to get away with this! *She* is the criminal!"

Bev looked at Mr. Feng angrily as another crew member took her by the arm.

The Countess' young companion ran up to Mr. Feng and fell into his arms, sobbing, even though the detective had a tight grip on him. "You and I were going to make a future together after the Countess died—isn't that what you said?" she cried. "You said we could divide the gold and run away together!"

The detective spoke to another crew member. By now a huge crowd of them had arrived, ready to deal with all the unsavory characters in the lounge. "Tell the ship's doctor that he should check the Countess' body for any evidence of puncture marks and confirm whether her key was still on her person," the detective barked. "And seal off both this man's cabin, as well as the Countess' suite. We'll get to the bottom of this gold that this young lady is talking about. Who knows, maybe we'll also find some aconite there, too!"

During all of this, Jack had the decency to look crestfallen, although Olive thought it had more to do with getting caught than any feeling of guilt.

She looked at the others. "Well, what about that double scotch? I'm still cold and I'm trying to dry out my clothes."

Weeping again, Maggie and Jean took her by the arm and led her to a table. The detective motioned for the crew members to take Jack, Bev, Mr. Feng, and the young Asian woman away, and then joined the women at their table.

Jean put her arm around Olive. "At least that blouse *still* looks fabulous! Just wait till you tell Howard!"

THE END

ABOUT THE AUTHOR

 Prior to retiring with her husband to Vancouver Island, Canada, L.V. Nield practiced law for many years in New York State. Working primarily in Elder Law, Laura was always aware of the vulnerability of seniors, resulting in the novel, *Kinfolk Killers—An Olive Reader Mystery, Book 1,* published in 2018.

Pleased with the response to *Kinfolk Killers*, Laura embarked upon this sequel, *Alaska Assassins—An Olive Reader Mystery, Book 2.*